Teller of Tales

A Musical Adventure from the
Life of Robert Louis Stevenson

Book and Lyrics by
Neil Wilkie

Music by
Neil Wilkie and David Stoll

A SAMUEL FRENCH ACTING EDITION

SAMUELFRENCH.COM
SAMUELFRENCH-LONDON.CO.UK

FOR PRODUCTION ENQUIRIES

UNITED STATES AND CANADA
Info@SamuelFrench.com
1-866-598-8449

UNITED KINGDOM AND EUROPE
Plays@SamuelFrench-London.co.uk
020-7255-4302

Each title is subject to availability from Samuel French, depending upon country of performance. Please be aware that *TELLER OF TALES* may not be licensed by Samuel French in your territory. Professional and amateur producers should contact the nearest Samuel French office or licensing partner to verify availability.

TELLER OF TALES

was first presented by
the Edinburgh Music Theatre Company at the King's Theatre, Edinburgh
12th July 1994

and by
the Forest Theater Guild at the Forest Theater, Carmel, California, on the
14th July 1994

CHARACTERS
(in order of their appearance)

LEERIE, a lamplighter
HOMAS STEVENSON, father of RLS
MARGARET STEVENSON, mother of RLS
BOB STEVENSON, cousin of RLS
CHARLES BAXTER   } Friends of
WALTER "WATTIE" SIMPSON   } RLS
First sailor
Second sailor
BETH, a prostitute
A publican
First constable   } Edinburgh
Second constable   } police
ROBERT LOUIS STEVENSON (RLS)
MAUD BABINGTON, another cousin of RLS
MRS. SITWELL, a clergyman's wife
SIDNEY COLVIN, professor and critic
A doctor
A nurse
A maid
FANNY VANDEGRIFT OSBOURNE
SAM OSBOURNE, her husband
BELLE OSBOURNE   } Children of Fanny
LLOYD OSBOURNE   } and Sam

First painter   } Friends
Second painter   } of Bob
Third painter   } and
Fourth painter   } RLS
An Irish girl
A horse-and-buggy driver
ADOLFO SANCHEZ, a saloon-owner
JOE STRONG, a portrait painter
NELLIE VANDEGRIFT, Fanny's younger sister
JONATHAN WRIGHT, a bear-hunter
JULES SIMONEAU, a restaurant owner

Ensemble of lamplighters, citizens of Edinburgh, editors, painters, models, crewmen, emigrants, townsfolk of Monterey, dream figures, diners, fictional characters
... and Modestine

SYNOPSIS OF SCENES

The action flows between Edinburgh and various locations in England, France, and California in the period from 1873 to 1880.

ACT I

ACT II

MUSICAL NUMBERS

ACT I

No.

1 "Old Town, New Town"....Leerie, Bob, Baxter, Wattie, Lamplighters,
and citizens of Edinburgh

2 "An Honest Trade"................RLS, Beth, publican, sailors and citizens

3 "Nothing To Question"..Thomas

4 "Adventure Is..."......................................RLS, Bob, Baxter and Wattie

5 "Circles"...Colvin

6 "Not This Child"..Fanny

7 "La Belle Americaine"....................................Bob and painters

8 Reprise: "Adventure Is..."..RLS

9 "Supernatural"..RLS and Fanny

10 Modestine"...RLS

11 "Time To Take A Chance"..................Fanny, RLS, Thomas, Margaret
Colvin and Mrs. Sitwell

12 "Better Days...................................Irish Girl and emigrants

13 "The Emigrant Train".............................RLS and emigrants

MUSICAL NUMBERS

ACT II

No.

14 "Ain't A Banker"....................................Driver, Adolfo and townsfolk
of Monterey

15 "What If I Did?".. Fanny

16 Musical fantasia:
   "Mountain Fever"...Dream figures

17 "Lay Down Low"....................................Jonathan Wright

18 Reprise: "Not This Man"...Fanny

19 "Fetch Me A Fandango"...........RLS, Belle, Fanny, Nellie, Adolfo, Joe
and Lloyd

20 "If I Live"...RLS

21 "Local Rag".....................................RLS, Simoneau, Adolfo and diners

22 "The Best Of Intentions"..Fanny and Nellie

23 "Making Allowances"...................................Baxter, Thomas, Margaret

24 "Reprise: "If I Live"...................................RLS and fictional characters

ACT I
Scene 1

(The city streets of Edinburgh. A January evening, 1873. As night falls several LAMPLIGHTERS are seen moving through the darkening streets, gradually illuminating a sombre backcloth which shows the two halves of the divided city. The first LIGHTS are lit among the wynds and alleyways of the Old Town (stage L), bringing into focus clusters of poor slum-dwelling CITIZENS huddling beneath crumbling Gothic towers.)

"OLD TOWN, NEW TOWN" #1

LAMPLIGHTERS.
LIGHT UP, LIGHT UP,
LIGHT UP OLD TOWN
EDINBURGH,
EIGHTEEN-SEVENTY-THREE.
WAKEN UP THE RATS.
LET THE BEGGARS SEE.
STUMBLING DOWN AND OUT
FROM CRUMBLING TENEMENTS,
ROGUES AND REMNANTS
MUSTER FOR THE NIGHT,
SKULKING IN THE STAIRWELLS,
GROPING FOR CHARITY,
HUNGRY FOR LIGHT.

(Other LAMPLIGHTERS now appear on the streets of the New Town (stage R) and in the glow of these gaslamps a number of well-dressed, prosperous CITIZENS are seen hastening to their comfortable drawing-rooms.)

LIGHT UP THE NEW TOWN,
GRACIOUS SOCIETY:
TIGHT WHITE COLLARS
AND STERN BLACK CLOAKS.
WATCHING CLOCKS
AND PREENING THEIR PIETY.
SHED ANOTHER BLESSING
ON THE GENTLEFOLKS.

(Both sides of the stage are now half-lit in the background by light from the several streetlamps. The foreground at R remains dark.)

OLD TOWN, NEW TOWN,
WITCHES' BREW TOWN,
CITIZENS DIVIDED
BY A BLADE OF GRASS.
THIS SIDE, THAT SIDE,
FIRST OR SECOND CLASS.

(Another lamplighter, LEERIE, now appears in the foreground of the New Town down R. HE pauses at one terraced house which is identified by a single light in an upstairs (third-floor) window.)

LIGHT UP THE NEW TOWN
  LEERIE.
STOP AT THE STEVENSONS',
EDINBURGH,
SEVENTEEN HERIOT ROW.
  CITIZENS.
WANT TO BUILD A LIGHTHOUSE?
ASK FOR THE STEVENSONS.
THEY CAN TELL YOU EVERYTHING
YOU NEED TO KNOW.

(While singing LEERIE has placed his ladder against the lamp-post outside the Stevensons' house and climbed up it. Now, as HE lights the lamp, THOMAS and MARGARET STEVENSON appear in the foreground approaching their house. LEERIE, unobserved atop the ladder, listens to the conversation of the Stevensons below. THOMAS, in his mid-fifties, a gracious and amiable man despite his thickset appearance and habitual grave demeanour of a Victorian paterfamilias, is clearly in a state of unusual agitation. HE carries a rolled-up white pamphlet in his hand. MARGARET, his devoted wife, has a naturally cheery disposition.)

THOMAS. I'll hae no more of it! He should be putting his mind to the law, not writing this sinful nonsense.

MARGARET. Och, it's just his high spirits, Tom. He's sae glad to be over the diphtheria.

THOMAS. His joking has gone to far, my dear. *(Flourishing pamphlet.)* There are things he's written here would make even a saint shiver. *(HE knocks sharply on the door of No. 17.)*

MARGARET. The puir lad's had so many illnesses, it's a wonder he has the strength to be writing at all.

THOMAS. The body's one thing, Margaret. It's his immortal soul that's in peril now. *(HE knocks again impatiently.)*

MARGARET. *(Shocked.)* Now, Tom!

(The door suddenly opens. As THOMAS ushers her ahead, MARGARET pauses on the threshold, playfully making an oblong shape with her fingers, smiling.)

MARGARET. Aye, ye'll be happy enough when ye see his brass-plate shining on the door. *(SHE taps him fondly and goes in.)*

(THOMAS follows MARGARET inside and we hear him calling inside the house. He and all the other characters pronounce his son's name throughout as "LEWIS".)

THOMAS. *(Voice off.)* Louis! Louis!

(LEERIE, climbing down the ladder, shakes his head. As THOMAS suddenly reappears in the doorway, looking mystified, LEERIE dodges out of sight behind the lamp-post. THOMAS calls to the top of the ladder.)

THOMAS. Leerie!   Have you seen my son this evening?   *(Mystified by the silence.)*   Och, is naebody where they should be?

(Visibly frustrated, THOMAS returns inside.   LEERIE emerges from behind the lamp-post and leans on it, smiling at his little trick.)

(At this point BOB STEVENSON, CHARLES BAXTER and "WATTIE" SIMPSON spring into view down the street and approach No. 17.   THEY are wearing the casually outrageous dress of students of their day, with long scarves trailing to their ankles, and are in high spirits, swigging from BAXTER'S whisky-bottle.)

BOB, BAXTER, and WATTIE . *(Together.)*
DRINK TO THE NEW TOWN!
PRAY FOR THE COMMUNITY!
HANG THE ROWDY STUDENTS
AND THEIR FIENDISH PRANKS!

(Unobserved by LEERIE, THEY whisk the ladder away.)

DRINK TO THE OLD TOWN!
LANDS OF OPPORTUNITY!
CLOSING DOWN THE BUSINESS
TILL TOMORROW, THANKS!

(THEY skip away, carrying LEERIE'S ladder.   As they do so, THOMAS appears again in the doorway of No. 17 and hails BAXTER, the last in line and nearest to hand.)

THOMAS. Ah, Charles! Have ye no seen Louis?

(BAXTER halts, hastily hides the whisky-bottle, and tries to assume a respectable lawyer's stance. Meanwhile, LEERIE, too late to hide again, sees BOB and WATTIE disappearing with the ladder towards the Old Town and sets off in pursuit, protesting.)

BAXTER. *(Looking up to the illuminated window of No. 17.)* Is he nae sunk in his studies up there?

THOMAS. He's not with that confounded nephew of mine, I hope.

BAXTER. Bob? *(Looking around for him.)* Och, no. Bob's away to a prayer-meeting.

THOMAS. Well, if ye happen to see Louis tell him from me I'm waiting to talk wi' him. Tonight.

BAXTER. I will that, Mr. Stevenson. And would you care to say what it might be about?

THOMAS. Aye. Liberty, Justice, and Rebellion.

BAXTER. *(Exclaiming aside.)* The L J R? *(HE gulps hard.)* Holy dram! *(To THOMAS.)* They're...er...easy words to remember. Yes, I'll tell him that, Mr. Stevenson.

(THOMAS turns and goes indoors. BAXTER looks alarmed.)

BAXTER. Hell's doorknobs - he knows!

(BAXTER rushes off to follow his friends into the Old Town, to the accompaniment of the students' musical theme. There, among the wynds at stage L, BOB and

WATTIE reappear, dancing and jesting with LEERIE'S and other ladders.   BAXTER joins his friends and breaks the news.)

BAXTER. We have to find Louis and tell him. His father knows about the L J R!

BOB. To the rescue! But, for God's sake, which one is he in?

(The chorus of LAMPLIGHTERS is heard again and LEERIE reappears, leading the search.   The LAMPLIGHTERS and other irate CITIZENS swarm behind him.)

LEERIE AND LAMPLIGHTERS.
OLD TOWN, NEW TOWN,
OLD TOWN, NEW TOWN,
OLD TOWN, NEW TOWN,
OLD TOWN, NEW TOWN,
OLD TOWN, NEW TOWN,
WITCHES' BREW TOWN:
DEMONS RUNNING RIOT
IN THE STREETS TONIGHT.

(The three students hastily place their ladders against a tenement wall, climb up and disappear. Old Town layabouts and beggars among the CITIZENS seize the ladders for themselves. Mayhem ensues as LEERIE and other LAMPLIGHTERS try both to recover their ladders and find the culprits.)

LEERIE.	**LAMPLIGHTERS.**
CATCH 'EM!	CATCH 'EM!
THIS WAY!	THAT WAY!

ALL.
BRING THEM OUT OF DARKNESS
INTO LIGHT!

(LAMPLIGHTERS and CITIZENS surge through the city, as the LIGHTS fade.)

Scene 2

("The Twinkling Eye", an Old Town hostelry. The tavern interior is dimly lit. In the centre is a crowded bar; in one corner, a curtained snug. Sailors, bedraggled women, petty thieves, and other sleazy characters throng the bar. Two smartly-dressed New Town gentlemen lean at the bar, surveying the company. A PUBLICAN dispenses drinks. Ribald jokes, curses, and drink flow freely. Two SAILORS, locked in argument, are bracing for a brawl.)

1ST SAILOR. Gang your ways, ye havering craitur!

2ND SAILOR. Keep your mou' stickit, ye saft-headed lubber!

1ST SAILOR. Ca' me a lubber, wad ye? Ye bandy-legged tarpaulin!

2ND SAILOR. Leave aff, ye skellie-eyed loon!

(From the snug BETH, a pretty Highland girl turned prostitute, appears. As SHE flounces confidently

toward the bar one of the well-dressed gentlemen makes a grab for her.)

BETH. Touch not, taste not, handle not!

(Her blunt rebuff with a temperance slogan provokes bawdy laughter from the gentlemen. Addressing the PUBLICAN, SHE gestures towards the snug.)

BETH. Twa mair drams, for him an' me.

(The PUBLICAN hands BETH two whiskies, and SHE heads back towards the snug amid further catcalls and laughter. Suddenly the hostelry door opens and several police constables burst in. There are protesting cries and groans from the company. All try to look sober except the two SAILORS, who are seized by one of the constables and carry on wrestling with him. The FIRST CONSTABLE moves to the centre of the action and issues orders.)

1ST CONSTABLE. Aff to the station wi' them. Drunk and disorderly.

(The SAILORS are finally separated, while the two gentlemen grab their hats and sneak to the door. As THEY go, a pickpocket lifts one gentleman's watch. The SECOND CONSTABLE sees this, grabs the pickpocket by the shoulders and himself pockets the watch.)
1ST CONSTABLE. An' we'll 'ave this one *(Pointing at the pickpocket.)* for thievin'.

(HE moves now to BETH who, still holding her two whiskies, is shielding the snug curtain. HE takes the whiskies, knocks them back, dumps the empty glasses on the bar and clamps his hand on her shoulder.)

1ST CONSTABLE. An' this one for questionable practices. And, of course, our host here *(Pointing to the PUBLICAN.)* for supplying excisable liquor to intoxicated persons. Right, be aff wi' them.

(As the constables make their arrests, BETH tries to wriggle free and calls out loudly to the snug.)

BETH. Velvet Coat!
1ST CONSTABLE. So! There's anither offender neukit in here, is there? Lets see what this one's up to!

(The FIRST CONSTABLE pulls aside the curtain of the snug. Instantly all noise subsides, characters freeze where they are, and everyone's eyes follow those of the FIRST CONSTABLE.)

1ST CONSTABLE. Well, here's a fine specimen for the magistrate!

(RLS is revealed, scribbling in his notebook at a small table. HE is exotically dressed in black velvet jacket, funereal shirt, yellow cummerbund, red-and-black scarf, and battered straw hat; around his shoulders, a broad swirling cloak. For some moments HE continues writing, then taps his notebook shut with a

pencil, looks up, gives the FIRST CONSTABLE a long cool stare straight in the eye, and rises from the table - a tall, spindly, raffish, instantly charismatic figure.)

RLS. Brazen buffoons! *(HE leaps over the table to face the FIRST CONSTABLE.)* Release these worthy citizens and pro bono publico stop the absurd theatricals! I have the written evidence to avert a most untimely miscarriage of justice.
BETH. That's right. You tellum, Velvet Coat!

(The constables appear to waver. The SAILORS shake themselves free. The pickpocket tries but fails to regain the stolen watch from the SECOND CONSTABLE. RLS coolly takes the arm of the FIRST CONSTABLE as if going for a constitutional, and walks him up and down.)

RLS. Know you not your Forbes-Mackenzie? The Act states that 'in duly licensed premises the populace may go about its business unmolested until the statutory hour of closing". Ergo the law may strike at eleven, but not, my friend, one second before. *(HE halts the FIRST CONSTABLE in their tracks.)* And the time is precisely - *(Leaping alongside the SECOND CONSTABLE and jabbing him.)* Ask him!
2ND CONSTABLE. *(Fumbling and pulling out the purloined watch.)* Five of eleven!
RLS. There you have it! In flagrante delicto est! *(HE calmly takes the watch, hands it to the FIRST CONSTABLE and addresses the whole assembly.)* So,

my quivering hearts of Midlothian, let business and pleasure resume in our precious palace of dreams. Publican, more whisky!

(The PUBLICAN pours several and gives one to RLS, who hands it to the FIRST CONSTABLE.)

RLS. Here, constable, accept a donation inter vivos and weet your thrapple! The burden of proof is now in your hairy hands. Voilà!

(BETH and the crowd chorus their approval, and SHE seizes RLS to give him a luscious kiss. HE savours and returns it, flinging his arms around her.)

1ST CONSTABLE. *(Thoroughly embarrassed.)* Fancy yesel' a clever chappie! Well ye've got four minutes. *(HE gulps the whisky and takes out his note book.)* For a start, Maister "Velvet Coat", who might you be?

(RLS breaks away from BETH. HE again takes the FIRST CONSTABLE's arm, and walks him up and down.)

RLS. Who would you wish me to be? The immortal bard? Montaigne? Dumas? Or Keats? Oh, that I could write as any one of these!
1ST CONSTABLE. *(Writing down.)* Immortal... how do you spell "Bard"?
RLS. I blush for you, sir! But let me tell you, I knew a remarkable constable once. Name of Barksby. Red-

haired he was, with rampant whiskers and a jagged scar across his brow. It was a freezing January night, and cutthroat rascals were on the rampage. Into the darkened alleys he leapt, whirling his truncheon to left and right. Blow upon blow struck home as a dozen rogues fell slithering to the cobbles.

(There are gasps from the bar-room crowd and constables.)

RLS. Barksby took one breath, and in that second, looking up, espied a welcome sign. A tavern - and a refuge! Quick as an eel he slipped inside. And here he smiled, for around him harmless humble citizens were quietly savouring their nightly medicinal.

(There are approving murmurs from the tavern audience.)

RLS. But Barksby wanted action.

(Excited noises from the listeners. RLS and the constables begin to act out the events as they happen.)

RLS. He sprang to a narrow window...

(RLS does so. The FIRST CONSTABLE follows.)

RLS. ...and there, overlooking the New Town, he beheld a spectacle of stiffening horror - a procession of sombre creatures, decked in frockcoats and equipped with monstrous weapons of ivory and silk and the very sharpest whalebone.

(The FIRST CONSTABLE draws back, reaching for his truncheon.)

RLS. A whole battalion of umbrellas. Sinshades!

(Noises of shock and horror from the listeners.)

RLS. Barksby knew his duty.

(The FIRST CONSTABLE readies himself for attack.)

RLS. He would root out these Deacon Brodies of the crescent, with their secret lusts, their bureaux stuffed with ill-gotten gains.

(All the constables are now poised for battle. The FIRST CONSTABLE crouches, ready to leap at the window.)

RLS. Yet that brave heart was seized too with tenderness for the lowly company around him.

(There are approving noises from the crowd.)

RLS. He reached out blindly for any bowl...

(The FIRST CONSTABLE does so; the PUBLICAN hands him a bowl.)

RLS. ...and dropped in a sovereign and a watch that was not his own...

(The FIRST CONSTABLE drops a sovereign and the purloined watch into the bowl.)

RLS. ...and swallowed one more tipple for the road.

(The PUBLICAN hands RLS another glass of whisky.)

RLS. Here's to duty and compassion, thought our noble constable.

(RLS and the FIRST CONSTABLE clink glasses.)

RLS. And never forget to love thy labour!

(The taverners burst into applause and congratulations.)

1ST CONSTABLE. This Barksby... he should be promoted. As for the likes of me, it's time I - *(HE checks the watch in the PUBLICAN's bowl.)* Strike me, it's past eleven o'clock! Fool me, would you, Mister Whatisname? You're no lawyer, you're a highway robber!

RLS. You have it right, the law is not for me. *(Spoken.)*

Grant me one digression
And take down my confession:

I, Robert Louis Stevenson, known to the bairns of the street as Spindleshanks and to my good companions here as Velvet Coat, do hereby declare that...

"AN HONEST TRADE" #2

I, NON COMPOS MENTIS,
APPLY AS AN APPRENTICE

TO BE A WRITER,
A TELLER OF TALES,
COMMANDER OF A READERSHIP
FOR RUNNING UP THE SALES,
THE CHEF WHO STIRS THE PLOT AROUND
AND SPRINKLES ON THE SPICE,
A PEDDLER OF PLEASURE
AT A REASONABLE PRICE
WHO NEEDS TO EARN A COIN OR TWO
BUT SETTLES FOR ADVICE,
A SOLDIER IN THE RANKS OF THE BRIGADE
WHO CARRY ON
AN HONEST TRADE.

YOUR HUMBLE POET,
BEGETTER OF VERSE,
IS SHARP AS ANY CARPENTER
BUT LIGHTER IN THE PURSE.
HE HAMMERS AT HIS SYLLABLES
AND CHISELS EVERY PHRASE,
THE ONLY MASTERCRAFTSMAN
WHOM THE PUBLIC NEVER PAYS
(NO WONDER SO MUCH POETRY

IS FREER NOWADAYS),
A JOINER IN THE PENNILESS BRIGADE
WHO CARRY ON
AN HONEST TRADE.

LOOK AT MY FRIEND THE PUBLICAN!
WOULD YOU SAY HE'S A THIEF?
   CHORUS. *(Chants.)*
NAH!
   RLS.
HE EMPTIES CASES FASTER THAN
A LAWYER DROPS HIS BRIEF.
   CHORUS. *(Laughs.)*
EHH!
   RLS. *(To BETH.)*
LOOK AT MY PAINTED DARLING HERE
WHO TURNS THE OTHER CHEEK.
   CHORUS. *(Sighs.)*
AHH!
   RLS.
HER POUNDSWORTH OF AFFECTION
IS THE BARGAIN OF THE WEEK.
   CHORUS. *(Swoons.)*
YEAH!
   RLS.
A LESS DISHONEST SPECTACLE
THAN THOSE WHO SNEER AT YOUTH,
WHO FEEL IT'S NOT RESPECTABLE
TO SHOW THE NAKED TRUTH.

*(The chorus makes noises of agreement behind RLS, who
   pulls out his notebook.)*

RLS.
HERE'S MY CASEBOOK, CONSTABLE,
BEHOLD THE FACTS OF LIFE!

(Thrusting the notebook into the FIRST CONSTABLE's hand.)

RLS.
TAKE IT TO READ BETWEEN THE SHEETS
AND ENTERTAIN YOUR WIFE.

AN HONEST WRITER,
A SLINGER OF INK,
CREATES WITH PEN AND PAPER
NOTIONS OTHERS ONLY THINK.
LIKE ANY OLD CAMPAIGNER
HE DEFENDS HIS POINT OF VIEW,
HE DOESN'T CLAIM THE MEDALS
WHICH ARE PLAINLY OVERDUE.
REMEMBER THAT THE DRAMATIST
COULD SHAKE A SPEAR OR TWO!
A PRIVATE IN THE PENNILESS BRIGADE
WHO CARRY ON
AN HONEST TRADE.

(BETH, the PUBLICAN, and all the tavern crowd join in the song and dance of celebration around the disgruntled constables.)

ALL.
TO BE A WRITER,
A TELLER OF TALES

COMMANDER OF A READERSHIP
FOR RUNNING UP THE SALES
   PUBLICAN.
THE CHEF WHO STIRS THE PLOT AROUND
AND SPRINKLES ON THE SPICE,
   BETH.
A PEDDLER OF PLEASURE
AT A REASONABLE PRICE,
   RLS.
WHO'LL MARCH YOU TO THE GATES OF HELL

(Groans from the chorus.)

   RLS.
THEN BACK TO PARADISE!

(Cheers of joy from the chorus.)

   RLS.
SPINDLESHANKS
HAS JOINED THE RANKS
OF THE PENNILESS BRIGADE
WHO CARRY ON
   CHORUS.
AN' ON, AN' ON, AN' ON, AN' ON
   ALL.
AN HONEST TRADE!

(As the song ends RLS is hoisted aloft in triumph, while the CONSTABLES are seized by exuberant taverners, carried round and dumped out of the door. The MUSIC continues softly as BOB, BAXTER, and

WATTIE appear through the door, gasping with astonishment at the scene.   THEY accost RLS and draw him aside.)

BOB, BAXTER, and WATTIE. *(Together.)* Louis!
RLS. The musketeers!   Where have you been, you traitors? You missed a merry escapade.
BOB. The grimmest news, cousin mine!
WATTIE. He's discovered it!
RLS. Who? What?
BAXTER. Your father.   He wants to talk to you tonight... of Liberty!
RLS. None too soon.
WATTIE. And Justice.
BOB. And Rebellion.
ALL FOUR. *(Together.)* The L J R!
BAXTER. *(Melodramatically.)* Prepare to meet thy doom!
BOB. The gallows call.
RLS. *(Turning to BETH, with an extravagant swirl of his cloak.)* One kiss before I die! *(HE takes it; the others applaud.)* And one for the road to eternity. *(HE kisses BETH again while his friends try to drag him away.)*
BOB. Hang one, hang the lot, say I. *(HE too steals a kiss from BETH.)*
RLS. Och, it's a bonny night to kneel at the block. I cannae stand on my feet.

(Half-drunk and staggering, RLS reaches out for support. To the final bars of the musical refrain, the friends carry him out amid cheers from the tavern company as the LIGHTS fade.)

Scene 3

(Thomas Stevenson's study, 17 Heriot Row. Long after midnight THOMAS STEVENSON, with white pamphlet in hand, is braced to confront his son. RLS knocks and walks unsteadily into the room.)

THOMAS. A fine hour for a youth to come creeping home!

RLS. A sudden turn of events. I was obliged to assist the police with their enquiries.

THOMAS. And what might be your excuse for this... *(Brandishing the pamphlet)* ...this wretched conspiracy?

RLS. I see you have unmasked the L J R. But what matter? We live in an age of new ideas.

THOMAS. Aye, and heresies. *(Quoting from the pamphlet.)* 'Constitution. Article One. Disregard everything our parents have taught us'! Och, Louis, lad, what fiendish creed is this you're scrawling?

RLS. They're not my words only, father.

THOMAS. A damnable secret society, eh? Is that it? Is that your game now? Or is it that artist cousin of yours who's taking you into hellfire?

RLS. Come now, father, you turn a skirmish into a battlefield.

THOMAS. Have ye no care for your mother and me in all this? Would you dishonour your own flesh and blood?

RLS. Honour thy father and thy mother. Aye, and love them too. Have I ever not? But where I go for pleasure must be my own affair. Besides, with the majestic sum of sixpence in my pocket I can hardly empty the family treasury.

THOMAS. If it's the coin ye'd speak of, ye know I've never denied ye that.

RLS. For fripperies. Umbrellas. But can't you see? Always your money, your prescriptions, your doctrine - or should I say theories?

THOMAS. It's these liberals are turning your brain. You're obsessed by that scoundrel Darwin.

RLS. Face the fact, father. Darwin does offer a credible view of the universe.

THOMAS. *(Urgently.)* Have ye no respect for the Kirk? The Kirk of your forbears, and your own?

RLS. *(With rising anguish.)* Has this family of engineers not had to search for answers?

THOMAS. *(Standing erect, face-to-face with RLS.)* Tell me the truth - do you call yourself a Christian man?

RLS. Why should I pretend? *(Unflinching.)* I reserve belief until I acquire further information.

THOMAS. That it should come to this - my son a back-sliding reprobate!

RLS. Our minds are free, father. You choose to spend your days measuring the power of storms and waves. I hear their soaring sounds and trace their changing colours. Times and men and circumstances move around us at a speed surpassing any hurricane. Yet you would have me planted in only one place, my head buried in only one book?! The whole idea is ridiculous.

That I should see like you... should be like you. A me
like you? Ridiculous!
    THOMAS. An atheist!
    RLS. A man must find his own answers!
    THOMAS. Answers?

*(At the height of their quarrel, Bible in hand, THOMAS
struggles passionately to assert his parental
authority.)*

"NOTHING TO QUESTION" #3

*(The song is sung by THOMAS. The rapid interjections
  by RLS are all spoken.)*

    THOMAS.
THERE IS NOTHING TO QUESTION, MY SON,
NO CAUSE FOR DEBATE.
I WOULD HAVE YOU REMEMBER THE FAITH OF
    YOUR FATHERS
BEFORE IT'S TOO LATE.
    RLS. Would you have me on my knees, bleating?
    THOMAS.
THERE IS NOTHING TO QUESTION, I SAY,
YOUR DUTY IS PLAIN.
PUT YOUR TRUST IN THE WORD OF OUR
    MERCIFUL SAVIOUR
AND SPARE HIM THIS PAIN.
    RLS. His word or his spirit? Christ never taught a
code of rules.
    THOMAS.
SUCH HOPE WE NURSED FOR YOU,

NO LOVE WAS GREATER.
MY PRAYERS WERE FIRST FOR YOU!
O, SEEK HIM, YOUR CREATOR!
   RLS. Speak not in the ears of a fool. Proverbs, 23:9!
   THOMAS.
THINK OF ONLY ONE QUESTION: "WHAT IS
THE CHIEF END OF MAN?"...

*(The opening words of the Catechism provoke RLS' final
bitter, frustrated explosion.)*

   RLS. When you hear a thing too often, you no longer
hear it!
   THOMAS.
"IT'S TO GLORIFY GOD AND ENJOY HIM FOR
EVER" ! ...

*(RLS walks briskly out of the room, leaving THOMAS in
anger and distress, still clasping his Bible.)*

   THOMAS.
IF YOU EVER CAN.

*(As the song ends, THOMAS looks sadly at the closed
door and buries his head on the Bible. The MUSIC
continues, played softly, almost as a piece of church
organ music, as THOMAS walks slowly to his desk,
sits, and opens the holy book. After a few moments
HE pushes it away in despair and his head bows over
his desk. Moments later we hear a light knock on the
door. MARGARET STEVENSON enters and places
an arm around her husband.)*

MARGARET. Whatever's keeping you here so late?

THOMAS. *(Rising from the desk, bitterly.)* We've got a reprobate for a son, Margaret, an accursed atheist!

(MARGARET is shocked. Instinctively SHE raises her hand over her mouth and closes her eyes to cover the tears.)

THOMAS. That's what the Lord's delivered us. And it's thanks to that degenerate nephew of ours, that Bohemian! That Bob!

MARGARET. But what about Lou, Tom - how are we to save him?

THOMAS. He's finished, my dear. He's chosen damnation, that's the end of him.

MARGARET. Maud Babington! My niece Maud! *(Seized with a bright new idea, her natural optimism immediately revives.)* We must send him to the Babingtons, Tom. To the rectory. See if a quiet stay with the Babingtons won't bring him to his senses!

THOMAS. Damnation... ? Or England? Aye, mebbe you're right. Better the devil you know!

(The LIGHTS fade.)

Scene 4

(Outside No. 17 Heriot Row. Some days later. The setting is as for Scene 1. It is late afternoon. From the doorway of No. 17 RLS emerges briskly into Heriot Row with a knapsack on his back, ready for the road. BAXTER enters from the other side and approaches him.)

RLS. *(To Baxter.)* The house is like a hospital. Gloom in every corridor. Stomachs turning over breakfast.

BAXTER. Invite me for a holiday!

RLS. My mind's made up, Charles. This is no place for a chronic invalid, with grim believers nursing me for heaven. If I am to write, I have to live - a real life, not the next one. So many Stevensons have shone their lamps, there must be one a sailor. Adventure, Charles! What else is worth the living?

BAXTER. Och, your brain's dried up with dreaming.

RLS. Death, after all, is the only certainty. It's the unknown that makes us truly alive. *(HE recites an impromptu limerick.)* Adventure be my teacher!/ I'll fight for the vagabond flag,/ Abandon the wig/ And the charlatan's rig!/ I'm ready to zig any zag. *(To BAXTER.)* Come with me, Charles. A partner in the enterprise!

BAXTER. I'd sooner shake hands with a lobster. *(Inspired by RLS, HE ventures his own impromptu limerick.)* Adventure is... a tunnel/ You enter it blind as a bat./ You're trapped in the stink/ With invisible drink -/ A rather bizarre habitat.

(During BAXTER'S limerick, which RLS politely applauds, from each side an unidentified figure has been backing towards them.)

RLS. Bravo, Charles. I applaud the rhyme if not the sentiments. Then you shall mount the rescue.
BAXTER. I'll stay here and keep the books. Counting the zeros.

(The unidentified figures suddenly turn and grip RLS and BAXTER on the shoulder, revealing themselves as BOB and WATTIE.)

BOB. Caught in the act of dispensing unlicensed banter!

(The foursome exchange greetings; laughter and horseplay.)

RLS. Brothers in liberty! You are here to witness and approve a radical departure. Mine. I stand at the gateway to adventure.
BOB. To France, Louis, with me! To the playgrounds of Bohemia! *(BOB launches into his own impromptu limerick, gesturing and posing melodramatically.)* Adventure is... a painting,/ The canvas awaiting my brush/ To stroke in a bed/ With a passionate red,/ And a violet caught in the crush.

(RLS, BAXTER, and WATTIE register disdainful applause - a slow handclap.)

RLS. *(To BOB.)* France, mon cher, must wait. I am obliged to call first on cousin Maud in sensuous Suffolk. *(HE ignores the other's groans.)* It's your turn Wattie. Give me a song for the road.
WATTIE. *(Ruminating in his customary fashion.)* I'm reminded of an old phrase...

RLS.	**BAXTER.**	**BOB.**
(Simultaneously.)		
Jump to it man !	Always waiting for Wattie!	He can't find his hymnal!

WATTIE. *(Deliberately.)* Faint heart ne'er wan fair lady. I say adventure is... a woman.

(This image excites them all. MUSIC starts.)

RLS. You have it, Wattie!

"ADVENTURE IS..." #4

RLS.
ADVENTURE IS... A WOMAN,
THE DANGER IN EVERY DESIRE,
A MESSENGER WHO
BEATS A SUDDEN TATTOO
AND SIGNALS HER MAN TO SHOUT FIRE.

ADVENTURE,
OPEN OUT YOUR ARMS TO ME!
BE MY GUIDE, MY
NATURAL SELECTION.

TURN MY GAZE ON
FARAWAY HORIZONS
AND EMBLAZON
EVERY NEW DIRECTION.
I DON'T NEED TO KNOW MY DESTINATION.
MY REQUEST IS FOR THE PLEASURE OF YOUR
     INSPIRATION.
TAKE ME, TAKE ME WHERE ADVENTURE IS
FOR ADVENTURE... IS A WOMAN.

ADVENTURE,
TITLE MY BIOGRAPHY!
TRAIN AND COACH ME
FAR BEYOND THE OCEAN.
I WON'T GIVE IN
WHEN THE SKY IS FALLING.
LET ME LIVE IN
LOVING LOCOMOTION.
THERE SHOULD BE NO CHEERS FOR MY
     ARRIVAL.
THE CHAMPAGNE'S ALREADY FLOWING FOR
     MY SHEER SURVIVAL.
TAKE ME, TAKE ME WHERE ADVENTURE IS
FOR ADVENTURE... IS A WOMAN.

*(Led by BOB, the four assemble themselves to form an
     impromptu barber's shop quartet.)*

BOB, RLS, BAXTER, AND WATTIE. *(Together.)*
SHE MAY SING TO YOU ACROSS THE SOFA.
SHE HAS LEFT HER SIREN DOWN BELOW,
SWEET AND LOW.

SHE WILL BECKON YOU TO THE PIANO
AND YOU KISS HER
PIANISSIMO.
*(RLS resumes his solo viva voce, stepping forward from
the others.)*

RLS.
ADVENTURE,
OPEN OUT YOUR ARMS TO ME!
HERE'S YOUR SHIPMATE.
SHOW ME TO MY QUARTERS.
CHART A COURSE THROUGH
PESTILENTIAL ISLANDS,
SAIL PERFORCE THROUGH
SHARK-INFESTED WATERS.
WE DON'T NEED TO KNOW OUR DESTINATION.
IT'S ENOUGH TO LEARN THE RUDIMENTS OF
NAVIGATION.
TAKE ME WHERE THE GREAT ADVENTURE IS
FOR ADVENTURE IS A WOMAN!

*(At the end of the song the last phrase is repeated as a
fading echo as RLS leads the others off and sets out,
knapsack on his back, on the pilgrimage to
adventure... and the LIGHTS fade.)*

Scene 5

*(The Babington's rectory in rural Suffolk.   Late
morning.   The setting suggests the grounds of the*

Cockfield Rectory: in the foreground, a carriage driveway leading to the Rectory doorway down L: at the rear a croquet lawn. RLS enters downstage R, with his knapsack still on his back, walking up the driveway at a brisk pace. HE is hot, dusty, and in a state of nervous excitement. From the Rectory steps his doting cousin MAUD BABINGTON rushes out to meet him, with a croquet mallet swinging in her hand. Some years older than RLS, MAUD is the Rector's wife: sociable and charmingly woolly-headed.)

MAUD. Louis, my dear, how thrilled I am to see you! Was the train on time? When I received your mother's letter, I wrote at once to a very dear friend I knew would love to meet you...

(While MAUD talks there appears in the Rectory doorway a mature, stunningly beautiful woman, MRS. SITWELL. In her mid-thirties, exuding poise and radiance even with a croquet mallet in her hand, SHE descends the steps gracefully to meet the newcomer.)

MAUD. ...a woman after your own heart... I mean in literature... as it were. And she said of course she'd tell Sidney and...

(MAUD'S fluttery tale has already been overtaken by events as RLS and MRS. SITWELL find their gaze riveted on each other.)

MAUD. *(MAUD turns to follow RLS' gaze.)* ... oh! There now... Mrs. Albert Sitwell... my clever cousin Louis from Edinburgh. Phew! Isn't this my lucky day?

(RLS, seemingly bowled over by MRS. SITWELL's presence, eagerly takes her hand and keeps holding it. Raising a provocative eyebrow, SHE gently extracts it from his grip. RLS looks thoroughly bewildered.)

RLS. I'm lost. Ye'll have to excuse a wee laddie from over the border who doesn't know a spouse from a sporran. Honest to God, Maud... *(Mimicking an ultra-Oxford accent.)* You do have a dashed jolly way of introducing a chap from - you know, that place with all the kippers!

(MRS. SITWELL beams broadly. MAUD giggles.)

MAUD. *(To MRS. SITWELL.)* You see how he is?!
MRS. SITWELL. I'm truly charmed Mr. Stevenson. Maud tells me you've been writing since you were six years old. You must be a very dedicated man.
RLS. Juvenile exercises, that's all I've done. Stowed away on family shelves, marked "not to be opened on the Sabbath". Dear Mrs. Sitwell, if I could only find a friendly tutor ... *(HE pauses, looking again straight into her eyes)* ...I would never leave her side.
MRS. SITWELL. Her side, Mr. Stevenson? But how surprising! *(SHE stretches out an arm to him, laughing.)* I would have thought... how interesting!

(RLS reaches out to take her hand. MAUD, already out of her depth and ill-at-ease, hastily seeks a diversion by swinging her croquet mallet at his outstretched hand.)

MAUD. *(Sweetly.)* Now, Louis, would you like to join the wives of the clergy at play?

(SHE produces a third mallet for RLS. The ladies start their game.   Drawn irresistibly towards MRS. SITWELL, RLS hovers beside her, fooling with the mallet while chattering excitedly.)

RLS. *(To MRS. SITWELL.)* I've tried my hand at historical works. Maud read my History of Moses when she wore a frilly pinafore and broke the fourth commandment on a garden-seat.

(MRS. SITWELL laughs and miscues her stroke. MAUD gulps.)

RLS. And essays.   I've written one called "The Modern Imagination". I'd write about women, but we don't have women in Scotland any more.
MRS. SITWELL. *(Again overcome with laughter.)* Mr. Stevenson! You're too much for me. But I know Professor Colvin will enjoy helping you.
MAUD. I wonder if his train is on time.
RLS. Professor... ?
MAUD. Sidney Colvin.   Slade Professor at Cambridge, a most influential gentleman in literary circles.

RLS. Sidney Colvin is coming here? The editor of "The Fortnightly Review" ? God bless me, whatever shall I say?

(Between his visions of MRS. SITWELL and COLVIN, RLS is at sixes and sevens. Totally distracted, HE misplays the croquet ball down the drive and hurries off in pursuit.)

MAUD. Wasn't I right? Isn't he a darling?
MRS. SITWELL. A bounding colt, my dear. And what exciting talent!
MAUD. Such a change from the churchwardens.

(RLS re-enters, carrying the lost ball in one hand and 'shouldering arms' with the croquet mallet in the other. With him now, side-by-side, is SIDNEY COLVIN. A smartly-dressed, earnest man in his late twenties, COLVIN is trying to keep pace with RLS' stride and flow of chatter.)

RLS. *(To COLVIN.)* Then I want to write a piece on John Knox. And one on Whitman, the great liberator. What spirit that man has, and such energy. Like a large shaggy dog baying at the moon!

(COLVIN greets MAUD and MRS. SITWELL and, unnoticed by RLS, give MRS. SITWELL an intimate squeeze of the hand. SHE whispers conspiratorially in COLVIN's ear, and THEY both listen attentively as RLS' monologue continues.)

RLS. And this England of yours, this - *(Edging closer to MRS. SITWELL and reaching for her hand.)* ...this gateway to adventure!

(MRS. SITWELL and COLVIN exchange embarrassed glances.)

RLS. These alluring country roads...

(RLS seems now to be not only excited but also emotionally disturbed. HE begins to hear 'inner' voices - pre-recorded and amplified throughout the theatre but evidently not heard by other characters on-stage - which encourage his accelerating infatuation for MRS. SITWELL. RLS' language and behaviour become increasingly eccentric, and as the scene develops it becomes apparent also that something more serious is amiss.)

BOB/QUARTET. *(Recorded voices singing, echoing.)* She may smile at you across the sofa...
RLS. ...Weaving voluptuously through undulating meadows...

(MRS. SITWELL lowers her eyes modestly. MAUD coughs nervously. COLVIN is bemused.)

BOB/QUARTET. *(Recorded voices singing, echoing.)* ...She has left her siren down below...
RLS. I started to write about them on the train. *(HE fumbles in a pocket for a notebook)* ...it must be in the other pocket...

MAUD. *(Agitated, interrupting in a loud whisper.)* You must understand, Louis, that Mrs. Sitwell is a somewhat wedded woman, though she may pray otherwise.

RLS. *(Oblivious.)* Aye here it is. *(Pulling out the notebook, HE quotes from it to MRS. SITWELL.)* "Sequestered loveliness!"

MAUD. *(Sharply nudging RLS.)* And Professor Colvin is her devoted admirer, as we say in polite circles.

BOB/QUARTET. *(Recorded voices singing, echoing.)* She will beckon you to the piano...

RLS. ... "the graceful curves of lonely lanes"... "their lithe contortions"... *(HE demonstrates the contortions with gestures and body movements.)*

(While COLVIN is amused, the ladies' eyes are popping.)

RLS. Och, I'll have to take off my knapsack! *(HE does so, dropping it beside MRS. SITWELL.)*

BOB/QUARTET. *(Recorded voices singing, echoing.)* And you kiss her...

RLS. *(To MRS. SITWELL, again quoting his notes.)* "You have to study nature systematically to enjoy her intimacy"...

MAUD. *(Desperately, sharply.)* Louis, it's your turn to play the ball!

RLS. *(Oblivious.)* ..."the exquisite sense of balance and beauty"...

BOB/QUARTET. *(Recorded voices singing, repeating.)* And you kiss her...

RLS. ..."every little dip and swerve"...

BOB/QUARTET. *(Recorded voices singing, repeating.)* And you kiss her...

RLS. *(Gazing into MRS. SITWELL's eyes.)* "Every gratification should be rolled long under the tongue"...
(COLVIN steps quickly between RLS and MRS. SITWELL, and gently draws RLS aside.)

COLVIN. Your imagination is remarkable, Mr. Stevenson. I suggest, however, that you rest your larynx for a while. Write about these romantic roads. Entertain us on paper. I'll find you a journal.

RLS. *(In a daze.)* You truly would? *(HE turns again to look at MRS. SITWELL.)* Then you, my lady, shall be my inspiration!

MAUD. *(Blocking his advance towards MRS. SITWELL, sharply.)* Louis! That is enough. Our friends have very urgent academic matters to discuss.

(MAUD ushers COLVIN away, takes MRS. SITWELL by the hand, and briskly escorts them off through the Rectory door L.)

RLS. *(Staring after MRS. SITWELL.)* She is a goddess!

(Left alone, RLS is beset by his 'inner' voices. Now they overlap each other, taunting and troubling him. HE moves about restlessly, struggling to contain his mental and emotional confusion while the montage of voices becomes louder and gathers pace.)

MRS. SITWELL. *(Recorded voice, echoing.)* I'm truly charmed, Mr. Stevenson...

BOB/QUARTET. *(Recorded voices singing, echoing.)* She may smile at you across the sofa...

MARGARET. *(Recorded voice, echoing.)* The puir lad's had so many illnesses...

COLVIN. *(Recorded voice, echoing.)* I'll find you a journal...

BOB/QUARTET. *(Recorded voices singing, echoing.)* She has left her siren down below...

THOMAS. *(Recorded voice, echoing.)* Disregard everything our parents have taught us?!

MRS. SITWELL. *(Recorded voice, echoing.)* Her side, Mr. Stevenson? How surprising!

BOB/QUARTET. *(Recorded voices singing, echoing.)* She may beckon you the piano...

COLVIN. *(Recorded voice, echoing.)* Your imagination is remarkable, Mr. Stevenson...

THOMAS. *(Recorded voice, echoing.)* It's these liberals are turning your brain...

MARGARET. *(Recorded voice, echoing.)* ... so many illnesses...

BOB/QUARTET. *(Recorded voices, echoing.)* And you kiss her...

MRS. SITWELL. *(Recorded voice, echoing.)* Mr. Stevenson! You're too much for me...

(As the montage of voices reaches its climax RLS claps his hands to his ears. When MRS. SITWELL's last phrase echoes through his head HE staggers downstage, sways and collapses. STAGE LIGHTS

immediately BLACK OUT, with the exception of a single SPOTLIGHT on his prostrate body.)

(The scene continues in the foreground, under SPOTLIGHTS only, to suggest that the action is not specific to any time or place. Lapses in time are implied by the pacing and LIGHTING of characters' movements.)

(A DOCTOR appears beside RLS and stoops to examine him. From the other side THOMAS and MARGARET STEVENSON enter. THEY are dressed in outdoor clothes. As THEY anxiously approach the DOCTOR there are slight signs of movement from RLS. The DOCTOR rises and takes the STEVENSON parents aside. The SPOTLIGHT follows the DOCTOR towards the parents, leaving RLS in the dark.)

DOCTOR. Extreme mental and physical stress, and - I regret to say - probably tubercular. He must go south, to warmer air. And he should go alone!

(THOMAS and MARGARET STEVENSON appear offended but relieved, turn to comfort each other and retrace their steps to the exit. The DOCTOR and spotlight follow them. For a few moments the stage is DARK.)

(Across the stage, in the golden and warmer glow of another SPOTLIGHT, RLS is now awake, propped up on a couch and writing vigorously. A NURSE appears beside him, shifts him to a half-upright

position and tries to tidy the sheets of paper on his lap. While RLS is protesting, a SPOTLIGHT on the other side illuminates the figure of COLVIN, dressed in outdoor clothes. HE is standing, chuckling, reading a manuscript.)

NURSE. *(To RLS.)* Mr. Colvin's here to see you again.

(The NURSE moves across to COLVIN, indicating to him to follow her in. COLVIN crosses briskly behind her. The SPOTLIGHTS merge. MUSIC strikes up, softly at first. COLVIN's voice is heard above the music as he returns the manuscript in his hand to RLS.)

COLVIN. "Ordered South" - I like that. Very promising, Louis. Yes. The tone is still uncertain, but the style - the style is pure gold.

(Encouraged by COLVIN, RLS moves to a sitting position on the couch. COLVIN promptly sits beside him.)

COLVIN. Put the illness behind you, Louis. London's literary circle needs your vitality. A fresh face, a new voice, a different accent - that's what they're looking for. *(Rising.)* You must meet some of our best editors without delay. And I know where to find them. *(Helping RLS to his feet.)* For congenial company and connections *(Taking RLS by the arm.)* there's no place like - the Savile Club!

Scene 6

(The Savile Club. The whole stage is LIT to show the decorated interior. As COLVIN and RLS enter together various gentlemen, PUBLISHERS, and other members of the Club, filter into view. To the traditional MUSIC of "The Flowers of Edinburgh". RLS is introduced into a magic circle of London's literati.)

"CIRCLES" #5

(The reel is played now at normal tempo. The verses, spoken or sung by COLVIN, are precisely timed to the rhythm of the reel danced by the gentlemen of the Club. Prompted by COLVIN from the sidelines, RLS joins the dance and follows his mentor's instructions on each new step in his career, distributing manuscripts as HE goes.)

COLVIN.
THE CIRCLE MEETS IN SAVILE ROW,
THERE'S EVERYONE YOU OUGHT TO KNOW,
I'LL SHOW YOU ROUND AND TURN YOU LOOSE
BUT FIRST I'D LIKE TO INTRODUCE

THE PUBLISHERS...
THE EDITORS...

CONTRIBUTORS
AND CREDITORS.

NOW SHOW YOUR PACES, TRY YOUR HAND
BUT START WITH THEMES THEY UNDERSTAND.
THEY'LL SEND IT BACK, THEY ALWAYS DO,
AND AFTER THAT IT'S UP TO YOU.

*(RLS plunges back into the dance, offering more
manuscripts to the reeling publishers.)*

COLVIN.
REVISE THE DRAFT AND CHANGE THE RHYME
THEN SEND IT ROUND A SECOND TIME.
MAINTAIN THE RHYTHM, KEEP ON SPINNING,
TRY THE END AT THE BEGINNING!

*(RLS promptly reverses direction, causing chaos among
the reelers.)*

COLVIN. *(Aside.)*
ESSAYS, POEMS, TRAVEL PIECES -
EVERY MONTH THE FLOW INCREASES.
THEN I MENTION MY CONVICTION:
    COLVIN. *(To RLS.)*
YOU SHOULD HAVE A GO AT FICTION!

*(RLS adjourns from the dance, mimes frantic writing of
new material.)*

COLVIN. *(Aside.)*
FASHIONING A LIKELY STORY,

BROADENING THE REPERTORY
KEEPS OUR BUDDING AUTHOR BUSY,
DRIVING LITERATI DIZZY.

(Several reelers stagger out of the dance, exhausted.)
    COLVIN.
THE SEASONS PASS, HIS EFFERVESCENCE
QUITE BELIES THE CONVALESCENCE
TILL ONE DAY, THE FINAL SPRINT,
AND WORDS OF HIS APPEAR IN PRINT.

*(RLS flings himself back into the reel, reviving flagging
    partners.)*

    COLVIN. *(To RLS.)*
CONGRATULATIONS! THERE I'VE SAID IT!
TRUE, NOBODY ELSE HAS READ IT.
NEVER MIND, WITH TIME AND TROUBLE,
WATCH YOUR CIRCULATION DOUBLE!
    COLVIN. *(Aside.)*
SO IT WAS. THE PROTÉGÉ
WAS OFF AND RUNNING ON HIS WAY
AND JOURNALS JOSTLED TO POSSESS
THE SIGNATURE... OF RLS.

(The dance ends in a tableau. BLACKOUT.)

Scene 7

(Courtyard of the Pension Chevillon, Grèz. Summer, 1876. It is early afternoon in the village of Grèz-sur-Loing on the edge of the Fontainebleau forest, south of Paris, France. A covered archway, up L, leads into the courtyard. A doorway, centre R, leads into the hotel. At the rear the courtyard opens onto a garden. In the foreground BOB STEVENSON is revealed, simultaneously at work and play. Clad in the colourful attire of a Bohemian artist of the day, HE leaps maniacally back and forth between his easel and a scantily clad MODEL.)

BOB. Just another minute, cherie! *(HE smothers her with kisses and adds a brushstroke to her torso before springing back to his canvas to dab a finishing touch.)* Et voilà! *(HE turns the canvas around triumphantly for the MODEL to see.)* A plumed ostrich in the mode of Millet!

(The MODEL screams, slaps his face, drapes a robe around herself and stalks off, up C, towards the garden. BOB shrugs. HE tosses the 'ostrich' aside, places an empty canvas on the easel and stands back to admire it.)

BOB. Now there's a masterpiece. *(HE fondly mauls the canvas, and calls loudly to the hotel doorway.)* Next!

(RLS enters through the covered archway L. With knapsack again on his back, HE now wears light striped summer trousers and a floppy hat. HE is in exuberant mood and carries a bottle of champagne.)

RLS. I fizz with joyful news!

BOB. Hallelujah, the reprobate!

RLS. My goddess flung me in the lap of the gods and they shower me with ambrosia. Colvin has opened wondrous doors. The editors are panting.

BOB. And the Venus in question?

RLS. She is the patron's own preserve. I leave them to their secrets. But pop the cork and I'll announce another miracle.

BOB. You've won at blackjack... the king of diamonds!

RLS. I passed my bar exams. *(HE hands the champagne bottle to BOB.)* For which my astounded father has pinned to my breast one thousand princely pounds!

BOB. Saints in aspic! *(HE pops the cork and fills two glasses.)*

RLS. My obligation is fulfilled. You see before you a free and thirsty man.

BOB. What a coup! To Liberty!

(THEY drink and pour again.)

RLS. Adventure!

(THEY drink again.)

BOB. The ladies of the bedchamber!

RLS. No more entanglements for me.   I'm off canoeing with Wattie.   We're here in Grèz only to assemble our accoutrements.   Our canal voyage will make my first book.

BOB. Louis! I have it! Your bounty must not stand idle. Supposing... supposing we buy a barge... we call her "The Eleven Thousand Virgins"... we paint her body with piping cherubs and -

RLS. Wattie, by heaven!

(HE sees WATTIE entering the courtyard under the covered archway, staggering towards them under a pile of camping gear which he drops at the feet of RLS and BOB.)

WATTIE. Terrible news, I'm afraid.

RLS. The canoes have sunk!

WATTIE. Worse than that. Rumour has it there are women painters at large.

BOB. In our blissful sanctuary? It's unthinkable.

WATTIE. Worse than that. They're - dare I say it? - respectable!

RLS. Unpardonable effrontery!

WATTIE. Worse that that! They're from "the other side". Americans!

RLS and BOB. *(Together.)* Americans?!

BOB. Colonizing us?!   They must be removed at once. Prepare the ambush!

RLS. To the boats, Wattie! Downriver! Encircle them from the flanks!

(RLS exits in a rush, upcentre, towards the garden. BOB gathers his easel and painting materials.)

BOB. I'll rally the troops. Man the ramparts! Enemy at the gates - in skirts!

(BOB rushes off R, into the hotel. WATTIE looks hopelessly at the pile of camping equipment, noisily gathers it up, and trundles off after RLS towards the garden.)

(After a pause, one by one an American family appears beneath the covered archway. THEY make a sombre scene. First FANNY OSBOURNE enters, dressed from top to toe in black. SHE is aged 36, below average in height, with naturally dark features; petite in an exotic way, mysteriously attractive. SHE moves in silence, restlessly, and looks unhappy. SHE is followed by her tall, fair, suavely handsome husband, SAM OSBOURNE, who is a few years older than FANNY. Running in behind him, their two children appear eager to look about and explore: BELLE OSBOURNE, a darkly pretty seventeen-year-old, and son LLOYD OSBOURNE, fair-haired and nearly nine. A MAID hurries past them into the hotel, carrying luggage. FANNY looks quietly about her, somewhat isolated from the others. BELLE and LLOYD lead their father around, taking in the scene.)

BELLE. Look papa - the roses and fruit trees... It's all so beautiful.

SAM. Vines, too, sweetie. Just like in California.

LLOYD. When can I start drinking wine, papa?

SAM. You have to wait a while till you're a man. That won't be long, son. Look at you now.

BELLE. Mama come! Down here! There's a big garden. And a lovely old bridge. Oh, mama, we'll have to paint that!

LLOYD. I wanna see the river. Where's my fishing-rod? Come on, Belle!

(LLOYD and BELLE disappear upstage. SAM's face clouds as HE watches FANNY move around, surveying the scene and ignoring him.)

SAM. They're gonna like it here, Fanny. They'll soon get over it. And you? What about you? Well, tell me - are you glad to be here or aren't you?

FANNY. *(Still avoiding his gaze.)* It's quiet and it's pretty. You'd better hurry, Sam, she'll be waiting for you.

SAM. *(Sharply.)* My friends are my business! Is that clear?

(LLOYD re-enters, running back to FANNY. BELLE follows him.)

LLOYD. Mama, come and see the river. It has real fish.

FANNY. Has it, darling? *(SHE looks at SAM for the first time.)* It's time to go, Sam. We don't want to hold you back.

BELLE. *(Taking SAM's hand.)* Oh, papa, why can't you stay?

SAM. *(To FANNY.)* What more can I do?

FANNY. *(Facing him, coldly.)* Go, Sam, go! Don't you think about it. We'll paint and fish. We'll manage. We'll send you sketches, won't we, Belle? We'll put on our loveliest smiles for the world. But go, Sam. Now. *(With a deep sigh, SHE turns away.)* I need to breathe.

(SAM moves to kiss her. SHE looks away defensively, allowing him only to kiss her cheek. The children look embarrassed.)

SAM. *(Crossing to LLOYD.)* 'Bye, son. Take good care of mama.

LLOYD. 'Bye, papa.

BELLE. *(Flinging HERSELF fondly at SAM.)* Oh, must you go so soon? There's so much to see. We could take boats on the river every day.

SAM. *(Hugging BELLE.)* Maybe next year, huh? 'Bye sweetheart.

(SAM looks once more, sadly, at FANNY, then exits through the archway.)

FANNY. *(To BELLE and LLOYD.)* Go along. Go change your clothes now.

BELLE. *(Petulantly.)* He's really gone now, mama. Don't you care?

(BELLE and LLOYD exit into the hotel, leaving FANNY holding their hats. BELLE's remark triggers a deep emotional response in FANNY, releasing her anger and despair as MUSIC starts.)

"NOT THIS CHILD" # 6

FANNY.
LET HIM GO BACK, THAT'S HIS WAY.
BUSINESS MATTERS, DON'T YOU SEE?
JUST LET HIM GO! LET HIM HAVE HIS DAY!
WHAT'S IT GOT TO DO WITH US? WHAT SHOULD IT MEAN TO ME?
HE WASN'T THERE WHEN OUR BOY WAS SICK AND AILING.
IMPORTANT BUSINESS. VERY OPPORTUNE!
AND WHEN AT LAST THAT LITTLE HEART WAS FAILING,
MORE IMPORTANT BUSINESS. "BE THERE SOON"!
OH, YES, WE WERE FOUR AT THE GRAVESIDE,
SHADOWS WEEPING IN THE RAIN
WE DIDN'T TALK. WHAT WERE YOU THINKING?
ONE LESS SHADOW TO MAINTAIN?
SO, BACK TO BUSINESS! SURE THAT'S FINE.
BUSINESS MATTERS. YOU HAVE YOURS, AND I HAVE MINE.

GIVING UP A HOME CAME EASY:
HANGING UP THE KEY, KNOWING PRETTY FRIENDS WOULD CALL -

THAT HURT CAN HEAL. A WIFE KNOWS HOW.
BUT HERE AND NOW IT'S MOTHER'S SHOW!
KEEP WHOM YOU WISH, I'LL NOT LET GO
(Hugging the hats of LLOYD and BELLE in turn.)
NOT THIS CHILD, NO! NOR THIS CHILD.

LIVING ON THE EDGE, AND LEANING:
FRIGHTENED OF THE FALL, REACHING FOR A
   HAND TO HOLD -
SO MANY TIMES I WATCHED ALONE.
I'VE LOST A SON, BUT THIS I KNOW -
THESE PRECIOUS ARMS I'LL NOT LET GO!
NOT THIS CHILD, NO, NOR THIS CHILD.

TO SEE HE'D STOPPED BREATHING!
SO SOON, SO UTTERLY!
THAT SILENCE - ENWREATHING,
STILL ACHING,
HEARTBREAKING -

WHERE'S MY PRIZE FOR CONSOLATION?
WHO WILL SHARE THE FIGHT, DARING TO DEFY
   MY SHAME?
WHAT WOULD I GIVE TO WALK WITH PRIDE!
(Looking towards the archway after SAM.)
GO TAKE YOUR LEAVE AND HAVE YOUR
   FLING.
TAKE ANYTHING!
MY WEDDING RING!
BUT NOT THIS CHILD,
NO, NO, NO, NO,
NOT THIS CHILD.

(FANNY hugs the children's hats tightly to her bosom. After a pause SHE looks up and shouts across the courtyard.)

FANNY. Go back to your fancy women, Sam, and let this one live again!

(FANNY strides off into the hotel R.   The LIGHTS fade slowly, to suggest time passing.)

(LLOYD enters the courtyard from the hotel, carrying his fishing-rod.   As HE runs with it towards the garden, the faces of various, young, male, oddly-dressed PAINTERS appear in unlikely places, spying, and grinning.   Two of them follow him off as a MAID enters from the hotel.   The others emerge to help her to set out a long dining-table and chairs.   As the MAID looks puzzled THEY crowd round to shush her and scamper away again to their hiding-places.   The MAID hurries away, alarmed, towards the hotel doorway.   SHE almost knocks over FANNY who emerges through the door carrying painting materials.   The MAID screams, curtsies an apology and exits in a hurry.   FANNY, having removed her outdoor clothes and hat, is still dressed in black. SHE is pondering where to set herself up for sketching when the spying faces of the PAINTERS reappear, watching her every movement.   FANNY looks puzzled, sensing their presence.   At this point LLOYD runs in again from the garden with his fishing-rod.)

LLOYD. What's happening, mama? Strange men keep saying to me: "Watch out, the Stevensons will get you." Who are the Stevensons, mama? Will they send us away?

FANNY. Whoever they are, Lloyd dear, they have me to settle with. We're staying right here.

(BELLE enters excitedly from the covered archway L.)

BELLE. Mama, have you heard about the Stevensons? Well, I've just met one of them. He looks like a gypsy, but he's so amusing!

FANNY. Belle, dear, we're not going to let them - Belle!

(BELLE, rushing back to the archway, careens straight into BOB. HE poses there, wide-brimmed hat in hand, flamboyantly garbed in yellow-striped stockings, a Machiavellian smile on his face. HE scoops BELLE up in his arms and whirls her in the air. While BELLE wriggles and giggles, FANNY screams, grabs LLOYD's fishing-rod, and starts beating BOB with it.)

FANNY. Put my daughter down at once, you savage!

BOB. Your daughter, madam, is quite a catch! *(BOB suddenly notices that FANNY is dressed in mourning. His tone changes instantly. HE lets BELLE down gently beside FANNY and stands back, surveying FANNY with respect and admiration, exuding charm.)* Ma foi! Mais quelle tristesse! I am alas a careless brute, and humbly crave forgiveness. *(Bowing low, with a dramatic* *flourish of his hat.)* Stevenson of Montparnasse at your command dear lady!

(BOB takes FANNY's hand and kisses it. This acts as a signal to prying PAINTERS around the courtyard fringes. THEY rush forward from their spynests, gather round and line up to be introduced. BELLE and LLOYD are surprised and excited. FANNY is unsettled by BOB's style, but soothed and mildly amused.)

FANNY. Stevenson. I have heard the name. I guess I'll accept the apology. I'm Fanny Vandegrift Osbourne. This is my daughter Isobel... my son Lloyd. We're from the United States of America.

BOB. I have heard the name. No apology necessary. And could it be the Goddess Art is your pursuit?

FANNY. *(Amused.)* Belle's the painter in the family.

BELLE. But mama, you've won medals.

(There are murmurs of admiration from the PAINTERS.)

FANNY. Our teacher in Paris thought we'd like it here. And you, Mr. Stevenson? Where is your native home?

BOB. On hills of debt, Madame. But we waste our time with smalltalk. *(Addressing the PAINTERS.)* Gentlemen, for our first lady from America, can we not do better that this? Let us conduct you around the estate. Le palais Chevillon has many classic features, besides its dazzling clientele. Consider, for example...

FANNY. Mr. Stevenson!   Before you go further, would you please tell me - are you one person or two?

BOB. Me? I'm inseparable. But wait till Louis gets here!

FANNY. He's your brother... ?

BOB. I am his elder cousin, and quite the least of his infirmities.   He suffers from fits of writing and an incurable strain of gibberish. Whereas I... when I see a work of art before me... *(Moving close to FANNY.)* I am reduced to rapt devotion. Such poise! Such timeless beauty! *(HE starts appraising her features at close quarters, and signals to the other PAINTERS to gather round.)* Can you not see, lads, the mystery of genius in the composition?

"LA BELLE AMERICAINE" #7

BOB.
MICHELANGELO DID NOTHING BETTER.
SEE THAT DELICATE BRUSH OF THE HAIR!
  1ST PAINTER.
YOU CAN TELL RAPHAEL HAD A HAND IN AS
  WELL
  BOB.
OH, A DOZEN OLD MASTERS WERE THERE!
LEONARDO, I THINK, DID THE SKETCHES
  2ND PAINTER.
BOTTICELLI JUST FOLLOWED THE LINE
  BOB.
BUT OBSERVE THE PRECIPITOUS DIP OF THE
  LIP -
THAT'S CERTAINLY NOT FLORENTINE.

I SUSPECT THAT THE EARS ARE VENETIAN
   3RD PAINTER.
THOUGH DOCTORED, PERHAPS, BY THE DUTCH
   4TH PAINTER.
THE NECK'S FAINTLY FLEMISH
   BOB.
THE NOSE IS THE BLEMISH -
THAT'S RUBENS, THE CAD,
SIMPLY LOSING HIS TOUCH.
THE GLOW ON THE CHEEK IS VELASQUEZ
   ALL. *(Sighing.)*
AH, VELASQUEZ!
   1ST PAINTER.
VERMEER MIGHT BE NEARER THE BONE
   BOB.
BUT THAT FINISHING GRACE,
THE ELLIPTICAL FACE,
COULD BE ONLY EL GRECO -
UNLESS IT'S HER OWN.
(To FANNY.)
MADAME, YOU UPLIFT OUR SOULS FROM
   DEPRAVITY.
ALLOW US TO SHIFT YOUR CENTRE OF
   GRAVITY.
(Grabbing a bottle, leaping onto a table.)
I GIVE YOU A TOAST!
IT'S AN HONOUR TO HOST
LA BELLE AMERCAINE!

(FANNY is amused by the flattery. As the MUSIC changes to pastiche-Offenbach BOB, the master of ceremonies, leads the song with frenzied exuberance.)

BOB.
TAKE YOUR SEATS! SETTLE IN,
LET THE CIRCUS BEGIN
FOR LA BELLE AMERICAINE!
   PAINTERS.
WOULD YOU SAY THAT PHRASE AGAIN?
   BOB.
LA BELLE AMERICAINE!
LOOK AROUND AND RELAX
WHILE WE COVER OUR TRACKS
AND TUCK THE BLACK SHEEP IN THEIR PEN.
BY A CURIOUS TWIST
THERE'S A FLOCK TO ENLIST
FOR LA BELLE AMERICAINE!

(WATTIE suddenly appears through the archway, still dragging his load of camping equipment. Nonplussed, HE drops everything and joins the dance.)

   ALL PAINTERS.
SAY THE WORD! NAME THE DEED,
AND AWAIT THE STAMPEDE
FOR LA BELLE AMERICAINE!
ASK A FAVOUR! TELL US WHEN!
LA BELLE AMERICAINE!
   BOB.
ANY TASK! ANY CHORE!
ANY FOOT IN THE DOOR,
A NOBLE QUEST FOR ABLE MEN!
WE'RE NOT HARD TO PERSUADE,

THE CRUSADE'S READY-MADE
FOR LA BELLE AMERICAINE!

*(While BOB and WATTIE ogle FANNY, the other
PAINTERS switch their attention to BELLE and take
her aside.)*

 1ST PAINTER. *(To BELLE.)*
WOULD YOU CARE TO SHOW THE WAY
THEY DO THINGS IN THE U.S.A.?
 2ND PAINTER.
ARE THE CHATTANOOGANS CHATTY?
 3RD PAINTER.
HOW MUCH SIN IN CINCINNATI?
 4TH PAINTER.
I'VE BEEN TOLD NEVADA'S HOT
BUT IS THERE NOT A HOTTER SPOT?
 1ST PAINTER.
HOW FAR DO WELLS AND FARGO GO
OR DID THEY STOP AT TEXAS?

*(BELLE and even LLOYD are drawn into the dance.
FANNY struggles to hide her amusement and
maintain her decorum, but continues to resist.)*

 PAINTERS.
IF WE TURNED OVERLEAF
 BOB.
WOULD SHE BE OUR MOTIF?
 ALL.
LA BELLE AMERICAINE!

BOB.
FOR AN ETCHING NOW AND THEN
  ALL.
OF LA BELLE AMERICAINE.
  PAINTERS.
BE A PAL! BE A SPORT!
  BOB.
LEND US MORAL SUPPORT!
STARTING NOW, WE'RE COUNTING TEN -

*(THEY count, in chorus, reaching nine before FANNY
    gives in.)*

  FANNY. *(Spoken.)* On one condition. No monkey-
business!
  ALL. *(Singing.)*
SHE IS NOT ONE OF THEM
  BOB.
SHE'S LA CRÈME DE LA CRÈME
  ALL.
LA BELLE AMERICAINE!

*(As the song ends, ALL collapse around the dining-
    table. Suddenly RLS springs through the archway
    into their midst. HE surveys the scene around him
    with astonishment.)*

  RLS. Have I missed the party?

*(In chorus the PAINTERS exclaim: "Louis!" Amid
    general uproar BOB leaps to his feet, panting an
    apology.)*

BOB. I was waylaid by a Mona Lisa!

RLS. I consider your betrayal disgusting and a good case for pistols at dawn. *(HE thrusts his knapsack into BOB's arms and moves towards the table. Catching sight of FANNY, HE at once removes his hat.)*

BOB. Tush! We have the most delightful guests. Mrs. Fanny Osbourne and gracious family... allow me to present my long-lost cousin Louis.

RLS. *(Bowing to FANNY.)* Madam, I scarcely expected such a pleasure. *(HE kisses her hand.)* But in black, Mrs. Osbourne! May a passing stranger offer sympathy? Your... your husband?

FANNY. My little boy... my youngest.

RLS. Then I pray for you, and all your dear ones. *(Bowing to BELLE.)* ...this charming young lady... *(And to LLOYD)* this likely lad o' pairts.

FANNY. Thank you for your kindness. *(SHE is pleasantly surprised by his courteous manner but it makes her nervous. Addressing the company at large.)* But please, we're not here to spoil your fun!

BOB. *(Clapping his hands.)* The wine, the women, the pot-au-feu!

(All take places at the table: RLS beside FANNY and LLOYD, with BOB and BELLE on her other side. A MAID enters from the hotel doorway and carries a pot-au-feu to the table. Food and wine are passed around amid the chatter.)

RLS. *(To FANNY.)* And what are you here for, Mrs. Osbourne?

FANNY. Peace and quiet. A change from the noise of Paris. To try forgetting these last unhappy months.

RLS. Forgetting, without your husband?

FANNY. Yes, Mr. Stevenson! Belle and Lloyd and I get along pretty well together.

BOB. *(Conversing with another PAINTER.)* C'est idiot! Monet calls it impressionisme. But the artist is the art. Look at Louis!

1ST PAINTER. What are you writing this summer, Louis?

RLS. The tale of our canoeing adventure. "An Inland Voyage", I shall call it.

2ND PAINTER. Fiction or non-fiction?

RLS. Most likely a shilling shocker.

BOB. With our hero wrecked in the first installment or this reader gets his money back. Young Lloyd here will settle the insurance.

(Amid the general laughter, LLOYD innocently joins in.)

RLS. Supposing we're seized by a gendarme and thrown into jail...

BOB. With a Rhinemaiden clinging to every bar...

RLS. ...the tenor bound with his own vocal cords, and the bass sinking inexorably to the bottom of his deep blue C. Think, Bob, supposing we lived in an opera. I open the bathroom door one morning to be clutched by a chorus of prancing peasants! Supposing -

FANNY. *(Rising to her feet, above the laughter.)* Supposing I were a trumpet and sounded the last retreat. I'm sorry, gentlemen, we must leave you. Lloyd should be in his bed.

(There are groans, cries of "Shame!" and applause for FANNY. BELLE and LLOYD rise reluctantly as FANNY turns to BOB.)

FANNY. Thank you Bob, for bringing fresh air into our lives.

LLOYD. And for not kicking us out.

FANNY. *(Turning to RLS.)* And of course, my thanks to you too, Mr. Stevenson. *(SHE muses, looking from one to the other.)* The two Mr. Stevensons. How are we to tell you apart?

BOB. Madam, be assured. I am only a vulgar cad, but Louis is a gentleman.

(RLS chuckles, says nothing, pats LLOYD on the shoulder, and escorts the Osbournes to the hotel door. LIGHTS fade on the rest of the group.)

RLS. Rest well, Mrs. Osbourne. The flowers of Scotland are at your feet.

LLOYD. Can we go fishing tomorrow, Mr. - er - Luly?

RLS. When I come back, laddie, with pleasure. Tomorrow I must set sail from this island paradise.

LLOYD. *(Breathlessly excited.)* From here, in a real ship?

RLS. A paddle-steamer. I'll paddle and my friend will steam.

(FANNY, BELLE, and LLOYD exit R, leaving RLS alone in a SPOTLIGHT. MUSIC starts. RLS flings his arms wide as he moves downstage into...)

Scene 8

(A canal bank in Northern France. Two canoes are in the foreground: the Arethusa - which RLS approaches, dropping in his knapsack - and the Cigarette, in which WATTIE now sits. Throughout the reprise sung by RLS the pair mime their journey through rain and floods, wielding paddles to the rhythm of the song.)

Reprise: "ADVENTURE IS..." #8

RLS.
ADVENTURE IS... A WOMAN,
A WONDERFUL SIGHT TO BEHOLD,
A VISITOR WHO
LEAVES A CLANDESTINE CLUE
THAT FORTUNE MAY FAVOUR THE BOLD.

(RLS steps into the Arethusa and the paddling begins.)

RLS.
ADVENTURE,
OPEN OUT YOUR ARMS TO ME!
HERE'S YOUR SHIPMATE.
SHOW ME TO MY QUARTERS.
CHART A COURSE THROUGH
PESTILENTIAL ISLANDS,
SAIL PERFORCE THROUGH

SHARK-INFESTED WATERS.
WE DON'T NEED TO KNOW OUR DESTINATION.
IT'S ENOUGH TO LEARN THE RUDIMENTS OF
   NAVIGATION.
LOVING LIVING FOR ADVENTURE
FOR ADVENTURE IS A WOMAN.
*(On the last word the canoes appear to collide. The
   MUSIC   stops   abruptly.   RLS   capsizes,
   "shipwrecked". WATTIE calls out.)*

WATTIE. Man overboard!

(BLACKOUT.)

Scene 9

*(Gardens of the Pension Chevillon. A warm afternoon.
Beneath white umbrellas, the PAINTERS are at their
easels.   There are sounds of twittering birds,
occasional whoops of distant laughter and a low hum
of voices lazily singing snatches of "La Belle
Americaine".   The atmosphere is erotic. In the
background, one painter casually sheds a shirt, leaves
his easel, and drifts away with an underclad model.
Elsewhere, BOB and another painter appear to be
vying for the attentions of BELLE: amid
expostulations and a mock display of fisticuffs
between the two, BELLE abandons her sketching and
saunters off with a suitor on each arm.   LLOYD
marches through the garden with his fishing-line*

stretched out behind him. WATTIE appears, with the fishing-line hooked to his midriff, and blithely follows LLOYD across the stage, juggling with a sizable and slithering fish. In the foreground FANNY, no longer dressed in mourning attire, sits at her own easel. As the stage is gradually emptied of other artists FANNY becomes impatient with her canvas and growls at it. At this point RLS appears in the background, apparently dry and wearing an Indian smoking-cap. Seeing FANNY alone, HE darts between umbrellas and creeps up on her. From above and behind, HE playfully covers her eyes.)

FANNY. Mr. Stevenson... *(Then in a warmer tone.)* Louis...

RLS. *(Smiling, dropping his hands and studying her painting.)* The waters under the bridge - nature could not do it better.

FANNY. I'm tired of landscapes. Will you sit for me, and talk?

RLS. Provided I may also write. *(HE sits beside her, takes out a notebook and pencil, and assumes a pose.)*

FANNY. I warn you now, my portraits are usually bizarre.

RLS. How pleasant! I can be myself.

FANNY. *(Sketching, studying him.)* You write so much, so many things. I have no doubt you'll be a great success.

RLS. Clairvoyance, my dear Fanny?

FANNY. Perhaps. It is a hobby of mine.

(RLS glances up at her, surprised and interested.)

FANNY. Please stay still. I'm trying to capture the author's genius.

RLS. *(Resuming his earlier pose, but restive.)* Fiddlesticks. I have no innate gift, it's damned hard work. I strive, I search, I scratch about, always to find the word that so exactly fits. It's carpentry. I know no other way. And with what result? A mere miscellany of periodic pieces. How can a man earn an honest living from such trinkets? Yet earn it I will, by God - or if not earn, then spend the less.

FANNY. You're too generous, Louis. You give it all away.

RLS. Why do you think that?

FANNY. I've heard it from your friends.

RLS. We do it for each other. *(HE rises unconsciously.)*

FANNY. Please, not yet! I almost have your eyebrow.

RLS. You may have one, if I may raise the other. *(HE moves around to peer over her shoulder.)* Oh, what a face! I wince to see my vanities exposed. *(Turning to look at FANNY.)* And you? Still shrouded in obscurity. America might not exist. Will no well-meaning words of mine entice you from your shell? *(HE puts his hand over hers.)* Won't you confide in me... a little?

(FANNY, unnerved, sets aside her sketching. SHE rises suddenly and paces about, summoning up her courage.)

FANNY. Oh, Louis - how does one begin? I hail from Indiana, so that makes me a Hoosier - you know, like whoseya friend? I married at seventeen and, yes, it started sweetly. My husband was private secretary to the State Governor - handsome, charming... and Belle was born. Three years later he went off to the Civil War, and we've been moving ever since. When he came back he started grubbing for gold. Oh, I've roughed it... slumming in mining camps, dodging the Apaches, trekking with Belle from one shack to another, waiting for her father to knock on our door again. And then he did, and Lloyd was born. Suddenly there was money... a cottage in California... a real home. But to my shame, I couldn't keep my husband. When our second little boy was born, the whispers and the absences became too much for me. Belle showed talent as an artist, so we took off for Europe. Antwerp... Paris, where little Hervey was taken ill and... And here I am. In a riverside garden with you.

RLS. But, how you've lived, Fanny!

FANNY. I've fought my battles. My parents called me Tiger Lily. I pack a pistol in my pocket still.

RLS. And yet, thank God, you can laugh! Oh, Fanny, you have nothing to fear from me.

(THEY look directly into each other's eyes a moment. Then FANNY turns away and picks up the sketchpad.)

FANNY. Your eyebrow isn't finished.

RLS. Finish me tomorrow. It's you we're just discovering. *(HE becomes keenly excited.)* Tell me now, do you believe in bogeys?

FANNY. Sure I do. My grandma kept closets full of them. When I was little she told me bedtime stories made my pigtails hit the ceiling.

RLS. Of ghouls and graveyards?

FANNY. Oh, yes. And screech-owls pouncing on the porch.

RLS. And ghosts of kings on horseback?

FANNY. Avenging headless housekeepers...

RLS. Wizards' woeful incantations!

FANNY. And giant teeth gaping over the parlour-door!

RLS. You must come to Edinburgh. Every family has a skeleton on the stairway. I've sketched a score of stories that would freeze the blood of a grenadier. But I never find the right ending. Perhaps I should write instead about falling in love...

(His last remark jolts FANNY and SHE drops her sketchpad. RLS gathers and hands it back. Aware that his words have struck a vital chord, HE continues fervently...)

RLS. Why not? What is more supernatural than love? The one illogical adventure. A heart which has been ticking accurate seconds all the year begins to bound and skip, racing beyond all reason. Passion runs wild. A woman smiles, and a man... stands moonstruck. He blinks, but still she smiles. They look into each other... *(His speech has slowed. HE and FANNY are looking straight into each other's eyes, hypnotically.)* And only this is absolute.

FANNY. *(Softly, slowly.)* Louis... how do you know these things?

RLS. *(Evenly, mesmerizing.)* I heard the willows weep at sunset. And frightened pigeons flutter from the storm.

(The LIGHTS have dimmed. The howl of an approaching wind is heard, a prelude to eerie noises. The beginnings of spectral MUSIC blend with the sounds of night. RLS and FANNY appear to be creating a mock-supernatural atmosphere around themselves to enhance their mutual attraction.)

RLS. Are you shivering too?
FANNY. I'm a little afraid.

(RLS draws FANNY closer to him. SHE appears to share the romance and fun of creating their own magic.)

"SUPERNATURAL" #9

RLS.
CHILLING BREEZES STRANGELY SWEEPING
NIGHTFALL INTO AFTERNOON.
FINGERS TINGLE, PULSE IS LEAPING:
IS NO PART OF ME IMMUNE?
SUN AND STARS ARE CHANGING PLACES,
LIGHTNING STRIKES WITHOUT THE THUNDER.
FEAR AND FEELING INTERLACE. IS
THIS YOUR WORK, THE SPELL I'M UNDER?
I'M SERIOUS,

FOR WOMEN ARE
MYSTERIOUS
PHENOMENA.

THAT FIRST BEWITCHING NIGHT EVENTS
   BEGAN
OMINOUSLY:
SOMEONE TOUCHED MY HEART AND
   WHISPERED
ANONYMOUSLY.
IN YOUR PRESENCE PHANTOMS BECKON ME
BACK TO THE CLUB.
I'M TOLD SHORT-SIGHTED MEMBERS LIKE TO
   CHECK ON ME:
"COULD THAT BE... ELZEBUB?"
MONSTERS NIPPING MY ANATOMY
SWEETEN MY DREAMS.
   FANNY.
VAMPIRE BATS DO THAT TO ME TOO.
   RLS.
ETIQUETTE BECOMES INFORMAL
IN THE GRIP OF THE ABNORMAL.
HERE AND NOW ARE
SUPERNATURAL.
ALL I SEE IS -

*(As HE is about to say 'you' and kiss FANNY, SHE
   breaks away and into the next refrain.)*

   FANNY.
SHAKING SKULLS WITH CROSSBONES
   CLATTERING -

FRIENDS YOU SHOULD MEET.
 RLS.
DRAGON'S BLOOD!
 FANNY.
WHERE?
 RLS.
SOFTLY SPATTERING
OVER YOUR FEET.
 FANNY.
COFFINS CREAKING, CORPSES QUIVERING
SCARE ME WITH JOY.
 RLS.
UNLIKE THE BODY SNATCHERS, QUICK
 DELIVERING:
THEY SCARE A SCOTTISH BOY!
I ATTRIBUTE TO A SORCERESS
MY ALTERED STATE.
 FANNY.
THERE'S A SAUCY TOUCH IN YOUR CARESS
 TOO.
 RLS.
LOCK YOUR DOOR AND DON'T UNDO IT!
 FANNY.
KNOCK BEFORE -
 RLS.
I'D GLIDE RIGHT THROUGH IT!
 BOTH. *(Together.)*
HERE AND NOW ARE
SUPERNATURAL.
ALL I SEE IS -

(As BOTH are about to say 'you' and kiss, THEY are interrupted by a ghostly scream. A dance - optional - follows, in which RLS and FANNY may be accompanied by phantoms and miscellaneous weird beings until...)

RLS.
HERE AND NOW ARE
SUPERNATURAL.
   FANNY.
PSYCHIC POWER!
   BOTH. *(Together.)*
SUPERNATURAL.
ALL I SEE IS YOU.

(THEY kiss. The spell is broken. Normal afternoon light returns. FANNY looks about anxiously, breaks from RLS, gathers her sketchpad and hurriedly exits. RLS remains as if hypnotized. The scene BLACKS OUT, except for a single SPOTLIGHT on RLS which is held into the early moments of the following scene. The same continuity device is used to denote the passage of time and changes of location through the series of 'vignettes' presented in Scenes 10-12...)

Scene 10

(Thomas Stevenson's study. The setting is as for Scene 3. THOMAS and MARGARET STEVENSON are

found with BAXTER. Across the stage, a SPOTLIGHT lingers briefly on RLS.)

THOMAS. It's not natural. He has his brass-plate on the door and never steps inside. You're a serious lawyer, Charles - is this the way to build a solid future for himself? I shall write and ask him that.

(The SPOTLIGHT on RLS fades out.)
BAXTER. *(Cheerfully.)* There's a choice of addresses this week. You might find him with Colvin in London. Most likely he's back in Paris. He has a lot of business there just now.
THOMAS. He's everywhere and nowhere.
MARGARET. He's busy with his writing, Tom. He's earned all of fifty pounds this year.
BAXTER. And sixteen shillings.
MARGARET. He's had the "Inland Voyage" published, and started his book on Edinburgh. Ye can't be asking more from him than that.
THOMAS. How can a man write about Edinburgh when he's capering around the streets of Paris? I tell you there's worse than writing on his mind.
MARGARET. And what would that be?
THOMAS. Witchery! Some Godforsaken foreign woman. One thing's certain - I'll be throwing no more good money after the bad!

(The LIGHTS fade, except for a SPOTLIGHT remaining on THOMAS, into...)

Scene 11

(The Savile Club. The setting in another corner of the stage, is recognisable as that used for Scene 6. RLS and COLVIN are locked in argument. A SPOTLIGHT still lingers on THOMAS.)

RLS. I need coin, Colvin, coin! Not compliments.
COLVIN. What more can a friend do? The magazines are full of you. The cheques are bound to multiply.

(The SPOTLIGHT on THOMAS fades out.)

RLS. Next year, next century!
COLVIN. Companions are expensive, Louis. You have no obligation.
RLS. I'm limp with overwork. Unless these foul publishers pay out their pittances, how am I to live?
COLVIN. It takes time Louis. The price of the profession.
RLS. To carve a tombstone would not take so long. I'd be in despair were it not for the loving head on my pillow...

(The LIGHTS fade on COLVIN and the scene, leaving only a SPOTLIGHT on RLS through the first moments of...)

Scene 12

(A railway station, London. The setting, in the central part of the stage, suggests the platform of a mainline railway station. FANNY, BELLE, and LLOYD enter downstage L. THEY are in outdoor clothes, struggling to carry various suitcases. RLS, still spotlit, stands down R, facing away from them.

LLOYD. Is Luly coming with us, mama?
FANNY. No, my pet, he must finish his writing.
LLOYD. When does Luly finish his writing, Mama? Will we ever see him again?

(RLS shows impatience, as the SPOTLIGHT on him fades out.)

BELLE. Luly was this year, stupid! We're going home and I'm glad anyway. I want to see my friends at last, and papa.
FANNY. *(Exploding.)* Stop it, Belle, you hear me?! Haven't you enjoyed yourself too? Haven't you seen my happiness? All right, it's over now and you're going home. But don't ask me to celebrate.
BELLE. *(Genuinely remorseful.)* I'm sorry, mama.
FANNY. The end of friendships I shall never forget... *(SHE picks up a suitcase.)* Come on, Belle, put your hat straight. Lloyd, did you pack your box of beetles?

(FANNY leads the children forward. Sounds of porters voices and a train whistle are heard. The Osbournes have almost disappeared down R, when RLS enters, running down L. HE calls and catches up with them.)

RLS. Fanny! *(HE pauses for breath.)* I thought I'd miss your train. *(HE embraces FANNY tightly, hurriedly.)* Here, I brought them both a souvenir. *(HE hands a small package each to BELLE and LLOYD.)*

FANNY. *(To the children.)* Hurry now. You go ahead and put the bags aboard.

BELLE. *(Coolly.)* Thanks, Louis. 'Bye. *(SHE exits R.)*

LLOYD. Gee Luly, thanks. Thanks for everything. *(HE gives RLS a warm hug, then exits after BELLE.)*

RLS. It's too cruel, Fanny, I cannae think straight! I cannae abide to see you go.

FANNY. You've work to do. A wonderful career ahead. There'll be no time to think of me.

RLS. But to go now! You know we'd still get by. On simple things.

FANNY. I've nothing left, my love, not a sou. If Sam hadn't paid the passage...

RLS. Och, Sam, Sam! What's he to you? Stay now and end the masquerade!

FANNY. I married him, Louis. I promised him my life. I have to try again.

RLS. Well, here's a Scot who'll no give in so easily. I'll think o' naething else!

FANNY. Just write, Louis. Your best. That's your life. Do it for me. Send me everything... whenever. Write me from France...

(A train whistle blows. FANNY breaks away from RLS, who turns on his heel as FANNY hurries off R. The voices of FANNY and LLOYD are heard calling.)

FANNY. Especially from France!

LLOYD. *(Voice off, calling.)* Where are you going, Luly?

RLS. *(Striding off.)* Walking, walking. You know how I like walking!

(RLS exits down L. The LIGHTS fade on the scene as, for a few moments only, the sound is heard of the train shunting away. This sound fades into MUSIC - another reprise of the theme for "Adventure Is..." - during the transition into...)

Scene 13

(A mountain trail in the Cevennes, France. The setting suggests wild mountain country. With the well-worn knapsack on his back, RLS strides briskly into view from stage L. HE turns abruptly, hands on hips, and walks back some steps to vent his fury at an unseen figure offstage.)

RLS. Very well, we go our separate ways. Yet, why, you witch? One moment you seduce me with that delicate smile, then presto! You retire to brood on some remote Atlantis. Well then, be off with you! My heart is cold as a potato. *(HE pauses, then shouts again* *offstage.)* God help us, what now, you rogue? Another shilly? Must I goad and prod and thwack you into submission? Then so be it, and enough of your petulant shenanigans! *(Striding off.)* Proot! Proot! Bestir your little shanks!

(MODESTINE, a diminutive donkey, enters L at a rush. It is only now apparent that she - the title-subject of RLS' current walking tour in the Cevennes - and not FANNY, is the immediate object of his wrath. Goaded by RLS, MODESTINE stops suddenly. The overfull pack-saddle slips, and its contents are scattered on the ground.)

RLS. Losh me, Modestine, could ye nae ha' waited till we'd said grace?

(RLS surveys the damage, repacks the saddle, and sings.)

"MODESTINE" #10

RLS.
MODESTINE, MODESTINE, MOUSE-COLOURED LASS,
I DIDNAE COME HIKING FOR YOU TO CHEW GRASS.
THERE'S MORE TO EXPLORE THAN THE COUNTRY CUISINE,
SO ADJUST YOUR CHAPEAU
AND LET'S GO, MODESTINE!

(With the packsaddle again in place, MODESTINE gives a jerk in the opposite direction, and pulls away.)

RLS.
DEAR LITTLE MODESTINE, OBSTINATE BEAST!
WHILE I'M TREKKING SOUTH, YOU'RE
  PROCEEDING NORTH-EAST!
I SCRAMBLE TO PEER AT A FABULOUS SCENE
AND WHAT DO I FIND?
YOU'RE BEHIND, MODESTINE!
THE VISIT I MADE TO THE TRAPPISTS
WAS SURELY UNWISE WITH A WENCH.
I HAD TO BEG PARDON,
THEIR MONAST'RY GARDEN
DEVELOPED A PERFUME DECIDEDLY FRENCH.

MODESTINE, MISCHIEVOUS MADEMOISELLE,
SEEMINGLY DOCILE BUT BORN TO REBEL.
YOU KICK AND YOU STAMP LIKE A PRINTING-
  MACHINE.
IF ONLY YOU'D WRITE -
WELL YOU MIGHT, MODESTINE!

RLS. I'll make a book o' ye yet, ye limmer! Your tantrums should raise a healthy chuckle. The irony of it, Modestine - to be lucky in print, unlucky in love. Eh, Tiger Lily! And where are you now, I wonder? D'ye spare me your dreaming once in a while? Tiger Lily... wi' your fiery tongue an' your loving heart. Och, love come back to me. Even an hour to share... even for just one kiss. *(HE leans forward tenderly, as if towards FANNY, but finds himself face-to-face with MODESTINE.)* You brute! *(Turning away crossly.)*

Throw the man out and have done! Oh, why did ye have to leave me?
MODESTINE, MODESTINE, MOUSE-COLOURED
    FRIEND,
WHERE WILL OUR TANGLED RELATIONSHIP
    END?
IN TORRENT AND TEMPEST OR CALM AND
    SERENE?
WE'RE AS CHALK IS TO CHEESE,
HE'S AND SHE'S, MODESTINE.
IT'S PLAIN WE WERE DESTINED FOR DISCORD,
THAT TROUBLES WOULD PEPPER OUR TRACK.
THE ARGUMENT WHETHER
WE STABLE TOGETHER
CAN HARDLY GO FORWARD WHILE YOU'RE
    GOING BACK.

THINK OF IT, MODESTINE, ONE LITTLE SHOVE
WOULD BANISH THE PAIN OF THIS FOOL WHO'S
    IN LOVE:
AND THERE IN THE MEADOWS WE TWO MIGHT
    BE SEEN
AS A GROOM WITH HIS BRIDE,
SIDE-BY-SIDE, MODESTINE.

    RLS. *(Calling out tenderly.)* Fanny, love! *(Lonely, frustrated and in despair, HE thwacks the donkey and stalks off, pulling MODESTINE behind him.)* Oh, come on, Moddy!

(BLACKOUT.)

Scene 14

(The Osbourne homestead, Oakland, California. In a comfortable cottage parlour, set upstage C, BELLE and LLOYD sit back-to-back: SHE at an easel, sketching, and he at a small desk, studying. LLOYD's hands are clapped to his ears to drown the offstage voices of FANNY and SAM, engaged in a heated marital quarrel. As FANNY enters from a side doorway, followed by SAM, the children try to ignore them.)

FANNY. I came back to you, didn't I?

SAM. You took your time.

FANNY. You've had your company. You didn't need me.

SAM. I do have a right to see my wife.

FANNY. But, Sam, you didn't need me.

SAM. Need? Why 'need', Fanny? I love you, always have.

FANNY. Like any goddam piece of furniture!

LLOYD. *(Shutting his book noisily, rising.)* How can I do my lessons when they're always shouting!

FANNY. I'm sorry, Sam, forgive me.

SAM. You're not well today Fanny.

FANNY. Or any day.

SAM. *(Cooling the atmosphere, addressing them all.)* I've rented a place for us all down in Monterey. For a couple of months. Sand, surf, and horses. *(Getting no* *response, HE turns to BELLE.)* Would you like that, Belle? *(Again without response, HE turns to LLOYD.)* And I'm gonna get you a pony. How about that? Come on out here, let's talk about it.

(BELLE and LLOYD, more cheerful, exit with SAM through the side door. Left alone, FANNY's anger and frustration surface immediately. MUSIC starts. FANNY is pacing restlessly as she sings. The MUSIC is sustained through all the spoken interludes.)

"TIME TO TAKE A CHANCE" #11

FANNY. *(Singing.)*
IF IT'S WAR, LET'S MAKE WAR!
COUNT THE AMMUNITION.
IF IT'S LOVE, SHOW ME LOVE,
NOT A CHEAP ADMISSION.
LET'S BE HONEST, SECRET SAM,
LOVE CAN'T LIVE IN HIDING.
LOVE IS PEOPLE POLES APART
SOMEHOW COINCIDING.
FANNY. *(Spoken.)* I'll take no more of this! *(SHE stops pacing, suddenly gentle.)* Oh, my dear, dearest Louis... how I need you now!
SCANDALMONGERS BLUR MY BRAIN:
"LADIES DON'T HAVE MEN FRIENDS"
BUT WE'RE TRUE LOVERS! WHY REMAIN
YOURS FAITHFULLY, JUST PEN FRIENDS?
FANNY. I must telegraph at once. *(SHE strides to the desk, scribbling quickly.)* There! *(Reading what

she's written.) "I've finished with him. Help me."
(Putting the message in an envelope and clutching it firmly.) Please, please, my tender, loving, dearest Louis... please come to me! You see I've heard your message. What is life without adventure?
IT'S TIME TO TAKE A CHANCE WITH A MAN
WHO TREASURES WORDS INSTEAD OF GOLD,
WHO'D MAKE MY LIFE A SENTENCE
I CAN LONG TO HAVE AND HOLD.
WE'LL START A NEW CHAPTER,
OPEN UP THE PLOT!
TAKE MY WORD WE'LL WRITE A GREAT
    ROMANCE
IF WE TAKE THIS CHANCE.

(Only a SPOTLIGHT remains on FANNY. Across the stage another SPOTLIGHT now illuminates RLS, in London, holding and apparently re-reading her telegram. The pulsating MUSIC continues. RLS is agitated. From the shadows BAXTER appears under the SPOTLIGHT, beside him.)

RLS. *(To BAXTER.)* The Lord knows what's in store for me, Charles, but I'm going. By the first available ship. *(HE hands BAXTER two letters.)* Here, one for my unhappy parents, one for Colvin. These will explain that I'm off my nut.

(With LIGHTS illuminating RLS and FANNY in opposite corners, the song becomes a "transatlantic" duet. RLS sings the main refrain, FANNY a counterpoint echo.)

RLS	**FANNY**
IT'S TIME TO TAKE A CHANCE WITH HER, MAN,	
AND HOPE THE HUSBAND'S' LEFT THE FOLD.	LOUIS... SOON...
IF HE'S REDUCED HER SENTENCE	SOMEHOW OUR TALE
I CAN COME IN FROM THE COLD	MUST BE TOLD...

RLS	**FANNY**
I'LL START A NEW CHAPTER,	A NEW CHAPTER
OPEN UP THE PLOT!	AND PLOT...
TAKE MY WORD I'LL WRITE A GREAT ROMANCE	A GREAT ROMANCE...
IF I TAKE THIS CHANCE	IF...

(A third SPOTLIGHT, in another quarter, reveals THOMAS and MARGARET STEVENSON, reading RLS' letter in Edinburgh. The MUSIC continues while THEY speak.)

MARGARET. Och, Tom, he must be ill again!
THOMAS. The humiliation of it! We shall have to leave Edinburgh.

(As THOMAS, then MARGARET, picks up the refrain, RLS and FANNY sing the counterpoint duet to each other.)

THOMAS
NO TIME TO
BREAK HIS
JOURNEY?
THE MAN
WILL BREAK
OUR HEARTS
AFORE HE'S
DONE.

THOMAS
THIS SINFUL
MAD
FLIRTATION
STAINS THE
NAME OF
STEVENSON

FANNY
LOUIS
...SOON

RLS
FANNY
...SOON

RLS/FANNY
...SOMEHOW...

SOMEHOW
SOON...

MARGARET
HE SAYS "... TO
WRITE A NEW
CHAPTER

POPISH DEVILS'
PLOT!
TAKE HIS WORD
AND PRAY
THE GOOD
LORD GRANTS
HIM ANOTHER
CHANCE.

OH, TOM!

OUR TALE
MUST BE TOLD...

FANNY
OH, LOUIS
SOON...

RLS
OH, FANNY
SOON...

(A fourth SPOTLIGHT now illuminates COLVIN, in London, reading RLS' letter with MRS. SITWELL beside him.)

COLVIN. He's out of his mind! He'll write nothing of value again.

(As COLVIN and later MRS. SITWELL takes up the refrain, THOMAS and MARGARET also sing in counter point. The song now becomes a sextet.)

COLVIN	THOMAS/ MARGARET	FANNY
THIS TIME HE COURTS DISASTER! THE MAN		
INTENDS TO RUIN HIS CAREER.	COME BACK...	LOUIS...
IF HE WANTS PUBLICATION	END THIS	
		RLS
THEN THE PLACE FOR HIM IS HERE.	ROMANCE...	SOMEHOW...
MRS. SITWELL	**THOMAS/ MARGARET**	**RLS & FANNY**
HE SAYS HE'LL WRITE A NEW CHAPTER,	CALL ON	OUR TALE
OPENING UP THE PLOT.	PROVIDENCE,	MUST BE TOLD...
COLVIN		
TAKE MY WORD THAT WON'T RAISE AN ADVANCE,	DON'T TRUST	... A GREAT
NOT THE SLIGHTEST CHANCE!	TO CHANCE.	ROMANCE.

(RLS and FANNY, till now far apart, come closer to reprise the last section of the refrain. The others, united in opposition to the lovers, sing in counterpoint as a quartet.)

RLS. AND FANNY
(Together.)

THOMAS/MARGARET/ COLVIN/and MRS. SITWELL *(Together.)*

WE'LL START A NEW CHAPTER,
OPEN UP THE PLOT,
OURS CAN BE A FABULOUS ROMANCE
IF WE TAKE THIS CHANCE OF A LIFETIME,
OUR ONLY CHANCE.

HE'S LOST THE CHANCE OF A LIFETIME,
HIS LAST, HIS ONLY CHANCE.

(When the sextet ends, the LIGHTS dim out on all except RLS. HE stoops to gather some books, puts them into a portmanteau, slings his knapsack over his shoulder once more, and prepares to board ship in ...)

Scene 15

(The emigrant's journey to America. The tale of RLS' journey - by ship across the Atlantic and by train across the U.S.A. to California - is told directly to the audience with RLS himself as the narrator. It becomes a kind of pageant, unfolding in story and song: a live documentary presentation of incidents and characters in RLS' travel-book which will only

later be written and published as "The Amateur Emigrant". The settings will reflect the changing locations of RLS' tale, which begins as HE steps up the ship's gangway. Once he is aboard and afloat, movements of the ship are conveyed by choreographic and sound effects. Crewmen and individual passengers come and go as RLS moves, strolls, sits or joins in the action according to the flow of the narrative.)

RLS. Youth is a hasty season. Chance drives me into a slantindicular second cabin of the S.S. Devonia. And here am I, amateur emigrant and passionate suitor, incognito, eager to unwind a sailor's yarn of how we pass our rolling hours and shifting days in this small iron country on the deep. *(HE moves from the gangway to mix with other PASSENGERS, finds his corner in second cabin, drops his belongings beside a table and chair, and studies his surroundings as the ship appears to set sail.)* Mingle with fellow Scots and Welsh and Irishmen and Danes, scrambling into steerage from their northern borders in a quest for - who knows what? a stronger brew? a different destitution? *(Identifying individual PASSENGERS as they come by.)* There's Isodor from St. Petersburg, rumoured squanderer of fifty thousand roubles, despatched to America by way of penance. And what of this antiquated lady off to Kansas, discarding some kind of husband, made for singularity. Even the colour of her seems incompatible with matrimony. *(HE is interrupted by the sound of the clapper on the brass and the BELLMAN's cry.)*

BELLMAN. *(Calling.)* All's well!

RLS. All's very well indeed, but... there's writing to be done. *(HE sits at his table.)* "The Story of a Lie"? "Pavilion on the Links?" Which of the tales tonight?

(As HE tries to work, assorted PASSENGERS watch in amazement.)

1ST PASSENGER. He's writing!
2ND PASSENGER. With a pencil!
3RD PASSENGER. What's he writing?
4TH PASSENGER. Look at 'im! Shakespeare!
RLS. That name won't leave me now. And nor will they.   One-hundred-and-twenty-eight uneasy bunks disgorge their occupants to gather at my music-hall.

(PASSENGERS mock him. A PURSER elbows his way through.)

PURSER. Wot's this, then? *(To RLS.)* So you're a writer, are you? That's 'andy. 'Ere, write me out this passenger list! *(HE gives RLS a sheet of paper and moves on.)*
RLS. Briskly done by Saturday... *(Rising, climbing a passageway to peer out)* ... when the wind freshened, the rain began to fall, and the sea rose so high a careless wanderer could disappear across the deck. *(HE pauses to listen.)* Another eight bells and -
BELLMAN. *(Calling.)* All's well!
RLS. On Saturday night, when the impulse to sing is strong... *(HE begins to sway with the tossing of the ship while PASSENGERS try to keep their balance.)* ... We

made a ring to support the women in the violent lurching of the ship, and sang and danced to our hearts' content...

(A FIDDLER plays.   The chorus of PASSENGERS breaks into the verse of a traditional folksong, and RLS joins in lustily.)

RLS. Until the bleak silence of the Sabbath...

(The FIDDLER's MUSIC fades.   The murmuring of prayers is heard.   The ship becomes steadier.   The PASSENGERS turn quiet.   RLS returns to his table and chair.   A male passenger walks by, furtively, observed by a tight-lipped, outraged woman passenger - and RLS.)

RLS. Prying eyes detect the sinful chessboard cuddled in an overcoat...
WOMAN PASSENGER. *(Looking heavenward in prayer.)* I'm surprised the ship didnae go doon!
RLS. But neither did the porridge...

(PASSENGERS are suddenly cheerful and animated. RLS rises again.)

RLS. Tuesday!   Fine skies encourage games and laughter ... Wednesday, arguments and memories ...

(A one-legged man with a crutch approaches RLS, tapping his arm.)

ONE-LEGGED PASSENGER. Smart as paint I was sir. But you see - I had a drunken wife! *(As HE hobbles away RLS scribbles in his notebook.)*

RLS. Emigration! There's nothing more agreeable to picture and nothing more pathetic to behold. Through the long wearying week, spirits rise and fall with the foam... until the dismal darkness drives my fellows down again to the vile stench of the steerage. *(Suddenly HE rushes to aid an ailing passenger.)*

SICK PASSENGER. O let me lie! O why did I come on this miserable voyage!

RLS. *(Hailing a crewman.)* Steward, there's a man lying bad with cramp and I can't find the doctor!

STEWARD. *(Unsmiling, disinterested.)* It's only a passenger.

(The bell claps again, followed by the familiar call - "and all's well!". RLS looks up to a passageway where several smartly-dressed passengers are taking a stroll, sneering at those down below.)

RLS. Above the agonies, others from well-appointed cabins pick their way with titters of indulgence. *(HE moves up towards them, then pauses.)* They sniff above the bulwarks, and I - ? I stare at a door marked "Gentlemen" and wonder if it opens now for me... *(Returning below.)* Day follows day, and dejection takes its toll... *(HE has to shout above wails and groans as the ship starts lurching heavily again.)* Lost, dog-sick and tongue-tied, where can they go? Unless to that friendly refuge, song?

*(The wailing begins to fade. MUSIC starts. Rising out
    from the melee of sprawling bodies, we hear the lone
    sweet voice of an IRISH GIRL.)*

"BETTER DAYS" #12

IRISH GIRL.
ON BETTER DAYS
THE SKY WAS BLUE,
THE LADS WOULD TEASE
AND TRY A SQUEEZE OR TWO.
THEN CAME THE ONE:
HE WARMED MY BED -
THAT PATRICK MOONEY!
NOW HE'S DEAD.
THE SKY WAS BLUE IN BETTER DAYS.

*(Her song slowly revives other PASSENGERS, who
    gradually join in.)*

MEN PASSENGERS.
ON BETTER DAYS
WE'D WORK TO DO.
WE'D EARN ENOUGH
TO SHARE ANOTHER STEW.
THEN THAT WAS GONE,
THEY THOUGHT IT BEST
TO HIRE A FEW
AND DITCH THE REST.
WE'D WORK TO DO IN BETTER DAYS.

IRISH GIRL.
WE'D STICK TOGETHER, HE SAID, AND I
BELIEVED.
MEN PASSENGERS.
THEIR TRICK'S TOO QUICK TO KNOW YOU'VE
BEEN DECEIVED.

*(A sudden shout stops the MUSIC. A YOUNG MAN
cries out, pointing through a porthole.)*

YOUNG MAN. *(Spoken.)* Look! Look! It's New
York! We've arrived!

(Others, including RLS, rush to look and start cheering.)

CHORUS OF PASSENGERS
TO BETTER DAYS!
1ST PASSENGER.
LOOK OUT AND SEE
THE HARBOUR WALL!
2ND PASSENGER.
MY BROTHER CALLING ME!
CHORUS OF PASSENGERS.
WE'VE COME INTO
THE PROMISED LAND!
LORD, GIVE US ALL
A HELPING HAND.
IRISH GIRL.
AND BE WITH ME -
CHORUS OF PASSENGERS.
AMEN

IRISH GIRL.
TILL BETTER DAYS.

(The MUSIC ends. The stage becomes a swirling mass of shouting, excited PASSENGERS rushing to land. RLS is lost among them. The background scene changes to suggest the port of New York, with a fresh hubbub of quayside noises and street cries. The crowd of PASSENGERS temporarily dwindles away as RLS steps forward to resume his narrative.)

RLS. New York! A rude and labyrinthine odyssey through banks and post-offices, railway offices and booksellers. I weathered every insult till the last, and lost my temper with a publisher. *(HE now appears to be weighed down with a load of books.)* By evening, with six fat volumes of Bancroft's History of the United States across my aching back, I was so wet that I could only divest myself of shoes and socks and trousers... *(HE does a partial quick change.)* ... and leave them behind for the benefit of New York City. I said farewell and reached out for -

(The crowd of passengers, now EMIGRANTS, surges back on stage. RLS struggles to find a way through them to resume his story. The action HE describes is again mimed and/or choreographed, as appropriate.)

RLS. The railroad! A block of passengers and baggage. A dense choking crush of laden humanity. Porters charged about like maddened sheepdogs. Children fell and were picked up, to be rewarded by a blow. One had lost her parents and screamed, as others pushed and ran. An official plucked her to his side... and I ran with the rest. *(HE does so, and stumbles towards the boxcar of a waiting train.)* We threw our bundles in the cars... *(HE does so, scrambling to grab a place.)* ... and squatted with our misery.

(We hear a WHISTLE, cries, shouts, and the RAILMAN's call.)

RAILMAN. All aboard!

(RLS sits between two young male EMIGRANTS, burly youths. With a deep sigh as the train appears to move off, HE resumes his story - but now more slowly, with a weary note in his voice.)

RLS. To witness this America with fellowship and oranges. I bought a cheap half-dozen. Only two could muster a pretence of juice, *(HE again takes out his notebook and pencil.)* And now I nod and stare and wonder, pulped by punishment and itching, through our melting summer days...

1ST EMIGRANT. Hey, Shakespeare, whatya writing?

RLS. Idle verses. Thoughts of America and this interminable journey. They might be your thoughts. Would you like to hear them?

2ND EMIGRANT. If they're not long words. I can't think long words.

RLS. The long words are Indian words. Beautiful words. *(Pointing.)* Like that valley. The Susquehanna. Susquehanna...

2ND EMIGRANT. How can anyone write Sus... que... sus? Bah!

RLS. I write. You listen.

1ST EMIGRANT. Go on, then. I wanna hear my thoughts so's I can think 'em.

(MUSIC begins. RLS reads aloud his lines for a poem later published. HE reads to the rhythm of the train, and of the song which follows.)

RLS. *(Spoken.)* "I think, I hope, I dream no more The dreams of otherwhere... I have been changed from what I was before; And breathed perchance too deep the lotus of the air Beside the Susquehanna and along the Delaware."

1ST EMIGRANT. Hey, that's amazing - my thoughts exac'ly.

"THE EMIGRANT TRAIN" #13

RLS. *(Singing.)*
MY TRAVELLING EYES ARE CLOSING ON THE
　　STREETS WHERE I BEGAN,
MY HISTORY HAS VANISHED IN THE AIR.
IN ITS PLACE I SEE THE FACES OF AN
　　UNFAMILIAR CLAN
GATHERED GRIMLY INTO BOXES BLOWN
　　ALONG THE DELAWARE,

HONEST BEGGARS DRUMMED ABOARD THE EMIGRANT TRAIN.
CHORUS OF EMIGRANTS.
THEY CAN SHUNT US INTO SIDINGS, WE CAN TAKE THE WEAR AND TEAR.
LEAVE THE BEGGARS ALL ABOARD THE EMIGRANT TRAIN.
RLS.
THROUGH ROLLING PENNSYLVANIA TO THE YARDS OF ILLINOIS
THE HERD OF HUMAN CATTLE RUMBLES ON
PAST THE CHAPELS OF THE FAITHFUL CHANTING MESSAGES OF JOY
AND THE WAVE OF FOLKS RETURNING, WISHING NOW THEY'D NEVER GONE,
MOCKING INNOCENTS ABOARD THE EMIGRANT TRAIN.
CHORUS OF EMIGRANTS.
AN' THERE'S THOSE WHO MADE A MILLION WHEN THEY PASSED THE RUBICON,
TIPPING BEGGARS ALL ABOARD THE EMIGRANT TRAIN.
RLS.
BEYOND THE GREAT MISSOURI, OVER BATTLEFIELDS OF FAME,
EVEN DIGNITY IS SLIPPING OUT OF SIGHT...

(Too exhausted to continue, RLS' head slumps forward onto his notebook. The dejected chorus picks up the song, and sings on as the train sways ever westward ...)

CHORUS OF EMIGRANTS.
WASH THE SICK AND COUNT THE WEARY,
    PLAY AN OPTIMISTIC GAME:
THERE'LL BE MOUNTAINS IN THE MORNING
    FOR SURVIVORS OF THE NIGHT,
HUNGRY BEGGARS ALL ABOARD THE
    EMIGRANT TRAIN.
PASS THE BOTTLE ROUND THE REFUSE, WE'RE
    ALREADY BLOODY TIGHT,
BROKEN BEGGARS ALL ABOARD THE
    EMIGRANT TRAIN.

(... and the CURTAIN FALLS on Act I.)

ACT II

Scene 1

(Into Monterey, California, and the Bohemia Saloon. A hot afternoon in August 1879. The scene is an empty landscape of sand dunes, bathed in the golden glow of a sunny afternoon. In the shade of the one visible scrubby bush a horse-and-buggy DRIVER, in broad-brimmed hat, leans against his cart. At stage R, an end-on view of a railway carriage reveals its steps. From the carriage a portmanteau is dropped down the steps, followed by a rug and, one by one, six identical fat volumes. The DRIVER watches as, behind the baggage, RLS steps into view. HE is in shirtsleeves and hat, with his black velvet jacket slung over a shoulder and his knapsack on his back. HE looks sick and exhausted. HE casts his eyes around, trying to understand where he is, and calls across to the DRIVER.)

RLS. Monterey?
DRIVER. Monterey.
RLS. Is this the station?
DRIVER. Monterey ain't got no station. This is Monterey.
RLS. Amazing! Not a house in sight.
DRIVER. Town's down the road. You a salesman?

RLS. No. More a man of letters.
DRIVER. You the mailman?
RLS. Alas, my friend, I bring only a sick and weary body, desperate for a ride to town.
DRIVER. Won't be the first one. Hop in.

(Another bearded local character, FIRST TOWNSMAN, enters. He sidles up to the DRIVER and nudges him quizzically, scrutinising RLS.)

DRIVER. Ain't a salesman.
1ST TOWNSMAN. So?
DRIVER. Ain't a mailman, neither.
1ST TOWNSMAN. So what is he?
DRIVER. Dunno. Says he brought a body.
1ST TOWNSMAN. Anyone we know?
DRIVER. Ask me somethin' easy.

"AIN'T A BANKER" #14

DRIVER. *(Singing.)*
HUSTLERS, BRAGGERS,
CARPETBAGGERS -
NEW FOLKS SNOOPIN' EV'RY DAY
STAKE OUT MONTEREY,
SIGN AND RIDE AWAY.

(While the DRIVER sings aside to the FIRST TOWNSMAN, RLS starts to assemble his baggage and books.)

STEALIN, SQUEALIN',
DOUBLE-DEALIN',
ALWAYS PUTTIN' ON A POSE.
TELL 'EM BY THEIR CLO'S.
ANY DRIVER KNOWS.

*(RLS slings his baggage on the cart and clambers in.
    The DRIVER picks up the reins.)*

TWO-BIT TRADERS -
NEVER MISS ONE!
ROVIN' RAIDERS -
LOOK AT THIS ONE:

*(The cart appears to start moving on its way L towards
    town. The FIRST TOWNSMAN walks alongside. RLS
    listens, amused and uplifted by the song.)*

AIN'T A BANKER. MAKE A BET -
ALL HIS BOOKS CAN COOK IS DEBT.
AIN'T A BROKER - ONLY BROKE.
GUESS HE COULDN' EVEN SWOP A JOKE.

AIN'T A COWBOY - GOT NO SPURS.
AIN'T A TRAPPER-
    1ST TOWNSMAN.
GOT NO FURS
AIN'T A MINER.
    DRIVER.
NEVER MIND,
WE CAN DO WITHOUT THE DIGGIN' KIND.

HE JES' MIGHT BE A PREACHER
  1ST TOWNSMAN.
LET'S PRAY HE NEVER ERRED.
  DRIVER.
BUT A SELF-RESPECTIN' PREACHER
WOULDN' HESITATE TO SAY THE WORD.

AIN'T A SAILOR, THAT'S FOR SURE!
  1ST TOWNSMAN.
AIN'T A SOLDIER - WHERE'S THE WAR?
  DRIVER.
AN' IF A SALESMAN'S LINE AIN'T HIS
  BOTH. *(Together.)*
I WONDER WHO THE HECK HE IS?!

(The DRIVER stops the cart, scratches his head, and turns to RLS.)

DRIVER. *(Spoken.)* Tell me, mister, you a settler hereabouts?
RLS. Certainly. How much do I owe you?

(As RLS searches for his purse, the DRIVER sighs, shakes his head, and jerks his cart forward again. Other TOWNSFOLK approach from several directions and walk alongside. The journey gradually turns into a festive procession.)

DRIVER. *(Singing.)*
AIN'T A SETTLER - NO ESTATE.
  1ST TOWNSMAN.
AIN'T A SQUATTER, CAME TOO LATE.

2ND TOWNSMAN.
AIN'T A WHALER - NO HARPOON,
  3RD TOWNSMAN.
AN' HE DOESN' SING A HUMPBACK TUNE.
  4TH TOWNSMAN.
AIN'T A BANDIT.
  CHORUS.
GOT NO GUN!
  5TH TOWNSMAN.
AIN'T AN OUTLAW
  CHORUS.
DOESN' RUN!
AIN'T A GAMBLER, ROLLS NO DICE.
  DRIVER.
SO HE'S GOTTA HAVE SOME OTHER VICE.

  1ST TOWNSMAN.
I RECKON HE'S A TEACHER.
  2ND TOWNSMAN.
HIS MARKS MIGHT GAIN A PASS
  DRIVER.
BUT A SELF-RESPECTIN' TEACHER
WOULD BE BETTER IF HE HAD SOME CLASS.
  CHORUS.
AIN'T A BOXER, AIN'T A PRO,
AIN'T AN IMPRESARIO.

*(The DRIVER halts the cart and addresses the crowd of
  TOWNSFOLK.)*

DRIVER. *(Spoken.)* So what kind of hick is he?

3RD TOWNSMAN. *(Singing.)*
AIN'T A WOMAN!
  1ST TOWNSMAN.
AIN'T MY MOM!
  CHORUS.
DOGGONE IT, WHERE THE HECK'S HE FROM?!
  DRIVER. *(Spoken to RLS.)*   Forgive me askin',
mister, would you be a Yankee?
  RLS. Just now, my friend, I'm incognito.
  DRIVER. Me too. Let's get us a drink and fast!

*(The DRIVER picks up the reins again and drives on. A
group of SENORITAS joins the procession.
Colourfully dressed, THEY laugh and chatter among
themselves and greet RLS coquettishly.)*

  1ST SENORITA. Hola, caballero!
  2ND SENORITA. Muy buenas tardes, señor!   *(To
her friends.)* Quien es?
  3RD SENORITA. No se. Vamos a ver!
  4TH SENORITA. *(Singing.)*
PALE AS A JAILBIRD!
  5TH SENORITA.
NAMIN' NO NAMES,
LOOKS LIKE THAT BROTHER OF JESSE JAMES.
  6TH SENORITA.
THIN AS A SPLINTER.
  SENORITAS. *(Together.)*
SKELETON MAN!
NEVER BE TOOK FOR A MEXICAN.
  5TH SENORITA.
RAGS ON HIS BACK.

6TH SENORITA.
SPOTS ON HIS CHEEK.
4TH SENORITA.
MUST BE A WANDERING CIRCUS FREAK.
1ST SENORITA.
TICKETS FOR SALE!
2ND SENORITA.
WELCOME THE CLOWN!
3RD SENORITA.
WHAT AN EVENT FOR THE TALK OF THE TOWN!

(The DRIVER pulls up sharply at the Bohemia Saloon, in Monterey's main street, which comes into view at stage L. Only a section of its clapboard exterior is visible, including a swing-shut door. The procession, and the MUSIC, stops abruptly.)

DRIVER. *(To RLS.)* That's it, mister. End of the line.

(RLS pays him promptly, with typical generosity.)

DRIVER. Gee thanks. *(Looking at the coins, astonished.)* A banker!
RLS. The Bohemia Saloon! Water in the wilderness.
DRIVER. Getcha somethin' stronger? *(HE calls inside.)* Hey, Adolfo! New gringo in town!

(The strumming of a guitar is heard from inside the saloon, greeted with shouts and a general hubbub of raucous male voices. The melodious baritone voice

of the guitarist rises strongly above the others, launching into a Spanish serenade.)

SINGER. *(Voice off.)*
AY-AY-AY-AY,
CUANTO ME GUSTA TU CARA! -

(More catcalls are heard from the Saloon. The singer stops. The sound of a pistol-shot is heard. The Saloon doors swing open. A customer hurtles out, does a kind of backward somersault, falls flat in front of RLS, slowly rises, dusts his pants and picks himself up.)

RLS. *(To the DRIVER.)* Who is that unfortunate fellow?
DRIVER. Some gringo.

(ADOLFO SANCHEZ emerges through the swinging door, carrying his guitar. HE is young, dark, and good-looking in a macho Mexican way. HE stands over the 'gringo', grinning.)

ADOLFO. I tole you before. You doan in'errupt when I sing a love-song okay?

(ADOLFO resumes his playing and singing. RLS listens, restless but intrigued. The verse is punctuated by more pained catcalls, growls and friendly mockery from inside.)

AY-AY-AY-AY,

CUANTO ME GUSTA TU CARA!
AY-AY-AY-AY,
NO ME DEJAS ASÍ, MI AMOR!
AY-AY-AY-AY,
ESCUCHAS MI POBRE GUITARRA -
AY-AY-AY-AY,
UN BESO PARA MÍ, POR FAVOR!

(The end of ADOLFO's song is greeted with ironic applause from inside. The crowd of TOWNSFOLK around him dutifully clap. RLS applauds ADOLFO with enthusiasm. At this moment JOE STRONG, a young, personable American-Bohemian artist, swings out through the saloon-door, with a glass of whisky in hand. HE is followed by other barflies.)

JOE. She's gonna love that one, Adolfo. The candle won't go out tonight.

ADOLFO. Is for Nellie from her nightingale. Is original, no?

(There are sighs and titters from the crowd. Suddenly JOE notices RLS, whom ADOLFO, in his romantic ardour, has ignored.)

JOE. Say, who's the stranger?

ADOLFO. Stranger? What stranger? Where is? *(HE sees RLS at last.)* Who is?

DRIVER. Picked him up at the railroad. Don't say who he is, but the guy pays cash.

ADOLFO. Pays cash - in Monterey? Eureka! *(HE shakes RLS warmly by the hand.)* Hola, hombre.

Welcome to Bohemia Saloon. I am Adolfo Sanchez. What you drinking, amigo?

    RLS. Please - a brandy... any brandy.

    ADOLFO. *(Calling inside.)* Best cognac for the gringo!

(A cognac is handed from the saloon. JOE gives it to RLS, who tosses it down.)

    ADOLFO. Now where you from amigo?

    RLS. Six thousand miles away.

(The crowd gasps. ADOLFO is stupified.)

    ADOLFO. Six thousand... ! *(HE calls inside again.)* Hola! Another cognac for my amigo! Is on the house. *(To RLS.)* You come six thousand miles to Monterey? *(Suspiciously.)* For what?

(The CROWD pushes forward to listen. Another cognac is passed out from the saloon, via JOE to RLS. The DRIVER's hand is still out, awaiting his own drink.)

    RLS. Looking for a friend.

(Another murmur goes round the crowd. RLS gulps his second drink and bends to confide with ADOLFO. JOE moves close to listen in.)

    RLS. Perhaps you could help me. I was told to ask for the Casa Bonifacio.

(ADOLFO and JOE react sharply. There are more murmurs among the crowd.)

ADOLFO. *(Exclaiming loudly.)* The Casa Bonifacio? Is impossible señor. Is where I sing beneath the window to my Nellie.
JOE. *(To RLS.)* You must have the wrong house. That's where my girl's living too. Who ya looking for?
RLS. *(Lowering his voice.)* Name of Osbourne.

(ADOLFO and JOE again react sharply. The crowd edges forward for more eavesdropping.)

ADOFLO. Be careful, señor. You mean Mister Osbourne?
RLS. No, no. Preferably not.
JOE. And not Miss Osbourne, 'cause she don't talk to strangers.
TOWNSFOLK. And not Mrs. Osbourne, 'cause she's a respectable woman.
DRIVER. So howzabout it, mister? What's your business?!

(RLS is confused, embarrassed and frustrated. Hemmed in by the suspicious crowd, HE draws ADOLFO and JOE aside for a blunt confrontation.)

RLS. Gentlemen, I have enjoyed our conversation. *(To ADOLFO.)* Your hospitality señor, does honour to Bohemia. But since my enquiries appear to disturb you, perhaps you could tell me where I could find a certain Mr. Joseph Strong?

JOE. Sure, I'm Joe Strong.

RLS. You? My forwarding address!

JOE. Then you're - *(HE stops himself just in time to avoid revealing RLS' identity to the crowd, and whispers to ADOLFO.)* It's -

ADOLFO. No! Is impossible. He's -

(JOE hushes ADOLFO just in time. THEY greet RLS with exuberant warmth.)

JOE. Welcome to Monterey, feller!

ADOLFO. Bienvenido, muy estimado señor!

(The three shake hands, and ADOLFO strums a flourish on the guitar.)

JOE. *(To RLS.)* You never told me you were coming! Gee, are you going to set the cat among our pretty pigeons. Come on, I'll take you to the Casa Bonifacio.

(RLS gathers his knapsack, and walks off eagerly after JOE, exiting L.)

ADOLFO. Cuanto mi alegro! Six thousand miles... por amor. Ay-ay-ay-ay... *(HE is about to resume his earlier serenade but is interrupted.)*

DRIVER. *(Edging forward with the crowd.)* So what's the story, Adolfo?

(ADOLFO reaches for his pistol and fires a shot in the air.)

ADOLFO. You doan in'errupt when I sing a love-song!

TOWNSFOLK. Come on, Adolfo, tell us! Who's the stranger? Who's the mystery man?

ADOLFO. *(Blandly resisting.)* Mystery? What mystery?

TOWNSFOLK. This mystery!

ADOLFO. Okay, I tell you what I know. But is confidential.

TOWNSFOLK. *(Loudly in chorus.)* Naturally. Everything's confidential in Monterey!

(The MUSIC of "Ain't a Banker" is heard again. ADOLFO leads the reprise.)

ADOLFO. *(Singing.)*
HERE'S THE LOWDOWN.
TOWNSFOLK.
BLOW BY BLOW.
ADOLFO.
IS FROM SCOTLAND.
TOWNSFOLK.
WESTWARD HO!
ADOLFO.
ON A GOOSE CHASE.
TOWNSFOLK.
WILD AS RICE.
DRIVER.
WHAT A CRAZY WAY TO PARADISE!
ADOLFO.
IS A CRACKPOT.

TOWNSFOLK.
SPILL THE BEANS!
   ADOLFO.
GETS HIS NAME IN MAGAZINES.
   TOWNSFOLK.
MUST BE FAMOUS!
   ADOLFO.
SAYS HE WRITES.
   TOWNSFOLK.
JUST ANOTHER OF THEM PARASITES.

   ADOLFO.
HE DON'T COME COURTIN' TROUBLE,
HE TAKES HIS LIQUOR STRAIGHT
AN' IF HE'S SEEIN' DOUBLE
IS BECAUSE HE MAY HAVE MET HIS MATE.

(A fresh wave of gossip runs through the crowd.)

   ADOLFO.
IN CONCLUSION -
   TOWNSFOLK.
PULL THE BRAKES.
   ADOLFO.
IS A CHARMER.
   TOWNSFOLK.
HOLY SNAKES!
   ADOLFO.
PLAIN AS DAYLIGHT, HE'S SINCERE.
   TOWNSFOLK.
BUT IF HE AIN'T A ROBBER, AIN'T A HOODLUM,

DRIVER.
AIN'T A CRANKY YANKEE DOODLUM
  TOWNSFOLK.
WHAT THE -
  ADOLFO.
HEAVEN HELP US!
  ALL.
WHAT THE HELL'S HE DOIN' HERE?!
(Tableau and BLACKOUT.)

Scene 2

(Parlour of the Casa Bonifacio, Monterey. The house is a traditional rose-decked adobe cottage off the main street of Monterey. The parlour is simply but tidily furnished with a dresser, several small tables and chairs, and a sofa spread with cushions. An outer door, upcentre R, leads to the garden and thence to the street. A second door, down L, leads to other rooms of the cottage. Three women of the Osbourne household are in the parlour: FANNY, BELLE, and Fanny's bespectacled younger sister NELLIE (Adolfo's fiancée), all engaged in characteristic pursuits. BELLE is sketching and looks dissatisfied. NELLIE, an avid reader and bookworm, is browsing in the pages of the local newspaper, the Monterey Californian. Both are lovesick. FANNY is busy preparing an evening meal while listening impatiently to the girls' idle conversation. BELLE jumps up, staring crossly at her sketch.)

BELLE. I hate this sketch. It looks like the jailhouse.

FANNY. What should it look like?

BELLE. The chapel. I think I'll go find Joe.

FANNY. Already? If you've finished sketching, chop these peppers. There's plenty of work for young ladies in this household.

BELLE. Yes, mama. *(SHE moves reluctantly to help FANNY.)*

NELLIE. *(Looking up from reading.)* Jeepers! It says in the 'Californian' this town's so poor they'll raise the tax on serenading another fifty cents.

BELLE. I didn't know Monterey was poor.

NELLIE. I didn't know Adolfo has to pay to sing to me.   That's awful.   Makes me feel like a sack of potatoes.

FANNY. Potatoes poppycock! If Adolfo pays your taxes before you're even married, you can be sure he really loves you.

(There is a loud knock. FANNY gasps. JOE puts his head round the outer door, upcentre R. BELLE looks delighted.)

JOE. Stranger in town asking for Mrs. Osbourne!

(JOE opens the door wide. RLS enters behind him.)

RLS. They tell me this is the haunted hoose. The one with the Hoosier!

FANNY. Louis! Great heavens, Louis! *(SHE rushes to embrace him.)*

(RLS is so weak and weary FANNY almost pulls him over. Their warm embrace embarrasses the young people: BELLE seeks JOE's hand, while NELLIE flutters shyly. FANNY senses the acute awkwardness of her situation and breaks away from RLS, trying to hide her confusion.)

FANNY. I don't believe it - here in Monterey! But look at you. So pale! However could you... no, tell me later. Come in now. Meet my sister Nellie.

(RLS cannot take his eyes off FANNY and watches her every movement anxiously. FANNY looks away, troubled. NELLIE edges forward nervously.)

NELLIE. Oh my goodness. It's so exciting for me to meet a real author. Fanny's told me everything about your books.

RLS. She has? Then she must be even cleverer than I thought. *(HE moves toward BELLE, who has stayed in the background with JOE.)* And who could forget this young lady?

FANNY. *(Agitated.)* Belle, honey! Won't you say hello?

BELLE. *(Coolly.)* Hello, Louis. I hardly recognized you. I guess I thought we'd never see you again. Welcome to Monterey.

RLS. Thank you. I'm surprised myself. It has been a long, long journey... a very strange experience. I propose to make a book of it.

FANNY. I want to hear you tell it first. Everything. But later.

*(The inner door down L opens.   LLOYD rushes in,
    straight into RLS' arms.)*

RLS. Weel, is it nae young Pettyfish - now a full-
grown salmon!
LLOYD. I've got a pony. Come and see!
FANNY. *(Sharply.)* No, Lloyd. Not, now. Can't
you see Louis is exhausted? There are more important
things he'll... *(Her voice dropping.)* want to know.
JOE. *(Sensing the delicate situation.)* I think we'll
step outside to tend the roses and LEAVE YOU TWO
TOGETHER. Come on, Lloyd!

*(JOE ushers BELLE, NELLIE, and LLOYD out with him
    through the garden door up C. Left alone, RLS and
    FANNY instantly turn to each other and embrace.)*

RLS. You see. I came to find you.
FANNY. Oh, Louis, no! What has this crazy journey
done to you? *(SHE is shocked by his exhausted and
tattered appearance.)* Look at your face, my love! And
you're so thin. *(SHE rushes to find refreshments.)* Here
-tea. Take it! Sit. And eat! Here - cookies. Oh my
darling, what an impossible pair we are.
RLS. *(Sitting and gladly accepting her offerings.)*
Cookies.   Fanny's own scrumptious home-baked
cookies. I feel better already. It's been a year, you
know, without you! The longest, most desperate year of
my life.
FANNY. *(Sitting beside him.)* I know, Louis. And
for me. But -

RLS. *(Warily.)* But? Buttered cookies? Wonderful. I'll have another.

(FANNY jumps up and starts pacing about, trying to pull herself together.)

FANNY. Oh, my love, I don't know how to - *(SHE breaks off, confused.)* Your writing - how's the writing? "Travels with a Donkey" - that's out now, yes?

RLS. Three months. Modestine is public property, braying from Pimlico to Philadelphia. Even teetering on a second edition. Unlike my book on Edinburgh - that only raises hackles at home and glasses in Glasgow. But you remember, Fanny, at Grèz, our beloved strolling minstrels... their terrible poverty? I wrote their story for the London Magazine and sent them my entire remuneration.

FANNY. No, Louis, no! You can't go on like this - giving, always giving. It's irresponsible. It's - oh, it's hopeless!

RLS. Not hopeless, just hard. I wrote another on the ship and sent it off to Colvin. And now, there's this appalling journey... "The Amateur Emigrant" I shall call it. Emigrant! The thought still amazes me... to have come here... to you... to stay. Oh, Fanny, love - *(HE rises and moves eagerly towards her.)*

FANNY. Don't, Louis, please. It's not like that!

RLS. What? You sent for me. *(Suddenly wary.)* He's not here, is he?

FANNY. We must find you a place to get well. There's a rooming-house on Tyler Street...

RLS. Fanny, tell me! He's not here?!

FANNY. No. But he'll be down tomorrow. *(With a kind of shrill hysteria.)* Oh, Louis, what am I to do?

RLS. Fanny, love, don't turn back now. You sent for me!

FANNY. Yes, yes, I did.

RLS. You said you'd finished with Sam!

FANNY. What if I did?

RLS. You've finished with him! You told me so!

(MUSIC starts. The first words of FANNY's song follow the dialogue without a break.)

"WHAT IF I DID?" #15

FANNY. *(Singing.)*
WHAT IF I DID?
MIDSUMMER MADNESS!
WHO TALKS OF MARRIAGE VOWS?
LOOK AT THIS SHAM!
DO AS I BID -
SEND ME YOUR ADDRESS.
STAND BY TO SALVAGE
THE WRECKAGE I AM!
TRY TO FORGIVE ME
THESE WOMANLY CAPRICES -
PLEASE DON'T COME NEAR!
NOT WHILE HE'S HERE.

RLS. So what happens now? We'd said if I kept faith you'd divorce him.

FANNY. You know what divorce means here for a woman? To be trampled in the mud like pigswill!

RLS. Then we'll go back to France together. At least you promised me that!

FANNY. *(Singing.)*
WHAT IF I DID?
SEE WHAT THE CATCH IS?
TWO MEN'S TOO MANY
FOR ONE HOMELY SOUL.
JUST LIKE A KID
PLAYING WITH MATCHES -
FLAMES I IGNITED
ARE OUT OF CONTROL.
TRUST ME IN ONE THING:
THE LOVING NEVER CEASES.
LOVE ME
AND LEAVE ME IN PIECES!

(FANNY breaks into tears. RLS moves to comfort her, but SHE stays distant, unresponsive. Slowly and sadly HE moves away.)

RLS. Is it the children? Aye, a child without a father is a melancholy sight. *(HE moves to pick up his knapsack.)* I'll go find myself a room to lay my things in. You know, Fanny, there's all kinds of fathers. Ye shouldnae forget I love your children too.

FANNY. I never doubted. Give me time, Louis. It isn't easy.

(RLS holds her tenderly and strokes her hair, then turns abruptly to the door up C and exits quickly. FANNY, distressed, seems about to call him back, then hesitates and turns away. LLOYD, BELLE, and

NELLIE troop back in from the garden. LLOYD runs excitedly to FANNY.)

LLOYD. Is Luly staying, mama? Will he come and live with us?
BELLE. What about papa?
LLOYD. That's all right, it's a big house.

(BELLE and NELLIE give LLOYD scolding looks.)

BELLE. Oh, stop it, Lloyd! I've had enough of Stevensons.
LLOYD. Luly's special. He tells the best stories.
FANNY. *(Her anger rising.)* Please, Belle. Louis has only just arrived.
NELLIE. And isn't he just so romantic!
BELLE. *(Snapping back at FANNY.)* What about Papa then? You said you'd make it up with papa!
FANNY. *(With a desperate, tearful shout.)* What if I did?!

(The surging musical coda of her song is heard again as FANNY hurries out, L, in distress. The others stand in shocked silence.)

(The LIGHTS fade quickly.)

Scene 3

(Above Carmel Valley. The setting is eerie. Backlit by a Pacific sunset sky and seen through a filter of breeze-blown fog, this is high hill country, a dozen miles from Monterey. The slowly darkening shapes of hill and hedgerow can be detected. The rasping click of cicadas and intermittent birdcalls can be heard. A male voice - it's JOE's - is heard close by calling "Whoa, there!", followed by the neighing of horses and the sounds of riders dismounting. RLS staggers into view, dragging camping-gear and coughing violently. HE is followed anxiously by JOE. RLS slumps onto a grassy bank and JOE kneels beside him.)

RLS. It's these infernal coastal fogs. They're worse than our damp Decembers on the Forth. I'll feel better in the mountains.

JOE. You're sure camping's the best medicine?

RLS. I know nothing. Mountains always clean my brain, but I know nothing. Thumped under the left pap for the woman of my life and shown the door by the resident philanderer - how my friends at home would wag their fingers now!

JOE. I bet the wind'll change when Sam's gone back to Oakland.

RLS. Perhaps. *(HE is caught again by coughing.)* No, it's nothing. *(The coughing subsides, and HE takes a long, deep breath to recover his composure.)* The fog's behind me, thank you.

JOE. *(Shuffling uneasily.)* If you think you'll be okay, I reckon I'll be riding back.

RLS. Go, man, certainly. I shall find my way ahead. Under the wide and starry sky, my friend, nature looks after her own. *(HE coughs again.)*

JOE. Even after dark? It's wild up here, you know.

RLS. Yes, yes, please go. I'd like to think a little.

(JOE exits quietly, as he came. RLS suddenly calls after him.)

RLS. It was a kindly thing to bring me on my way! *(Musing to himself.)* "For I am very lucky with a lamp..." *(HE rises, gathers up his camping-gear and prepares to move on, reciting a snatch of his own verse.)* "The air was still, the water ran, / No need was there for maid or man ..." *(HE stops to ponder.)* No need? Ah, dear Modestine, mouse-coloured friend, where will our tangled relationship end? *(Thinking only of FANNY, HE sings to himself - unaccompanied.)*
THINK OF IT, MODESTINE, ONE LITTLE SHOVE
WOULD BANISH THE PAIN OF THIS FOOL ...
(HE breaks off singing, with a cry of anguish) - who's in love!

(RLS moves on. HE appears now to be climbing further up into the mountains, a silhouette behind a gauze. Prompted by the eeriness of his surroundings and the

sounds of the wild, he sings to himself - again unaccompanied - a verse from his 'song for the road')

RLS.
ADVENTURE,
TITLE MY BIOGRAPHY!
TRAIN AND COACH ME
FAR BEYOND THE OCEAN.
I WON'T GIVE IN
WHEN THE SKY IS FALLING -

(The verse breaks off. We hear the sounds of tree-frogs croaking and intermittent goat-bells ringing. The figure of RLS now comes into full view again in the foreground. MUSIC starts, gradually becoming louder. It is the animating force of the emerging scene in which the action is portrayed only through mime and choreography.)

Musical Fantasia - "MOUNTAIN FEVER" #16

(RLS looks up, shivers, sets down his lamp, starts coughing, fumbles to make a campfire to brew tea, becomes agitated and scrambles to unfold a sleeping-bag. There is only a dim LIGHT around him. HE covers himself, but once into the sleeping-bag we see that he can't sleep. HE tosses and turns and flails about, apparently feverish. The musical theme of "Circles" which we first hear merges into other themes associated with key moments in his life. Gradually the optimistic themes fade out and the

fantasia becomes more dramatic as RLS, writhing restlessly, is assailed by devastating nightmares...

In the background, illuminated now by the recurrent flashing of a revolving lighthouse lamp, spectral figures emerge - among them a slim and agile figure in a black velvet jacket, the 'dream' RLS who is the centre-piece of a 'mountain fever' ballet in which both factual and fictional figures now take part. As the real RLS tosses and turns and we enter the world of his dream, the stage is bathed in a brilliant, drenching light...

The figure of THOMAS STEVENSON appears in a pulpit. Looking like a fiery John Knox, he preaches a sermon at the dream RLS, who swings away to join a group of Scottish Covenanters marching past THOMAS and going into battle. MARGARET STEVENSON is rocking a cradle, where the dream RLS crouches to rest his head. Respectable Edinburgh citizens gather round and rock the cradle with MARGARET, but when THEY move away the RLS figure is no longer there...

Pirate figures appear, joined by the figures of BOB, BAXTER, and WATTIE dancing a few bars of a hornpipe. The RLS figure is running to catch up, but when they pass THOMAS' pulpit the others dance away and RLS is trapped again. HE is seized by two bewigged judges. They place a wig on RLS and march him off to court, where they preside over the apparent trial of two umbrellas. As these are snapped shut, they reveal COLVIN and MRS. SITWELL. The judges disappear. The RLS figure, snubbing COLVIN, gazes adoringly at MRS. SITWELL...

A third white umbrella appears, closes and reveals the figure of FANNY, who kicks COLVIN aside and faces MRS. SITWELL eyeball to eyeball. RLS chases FANNY, and MRS. SITWELL disappears. But RLS and FANNY are again trapped by THOMAS sermonizing. They run to MARGARET but she, still placidly rocking on the cradle, ignores them...

Suddenly, behind THOMAS and conjured up by him, there appears the figure of the DEVIL, who pursues RLS and FANNY. SHE pulls out a pistol, tries to shoot the DEVIL, but instead hits the dream RLS in the heart. As HE falls, the DEVIL leaps to hover over the real, writhing RLS. As the DEVIL reaches out to seize him, the figures of THOMAS, MARGARET, and FANNY freeze. The real RLS sits up sharply and cries out chillingly -)

RLS. I've swallowed the world!

(HE falls back as if dead. Instantly the dramatic MUSIC stops, all dream FIGURES appear, and the lighting reverts to its former faint glow over RLS in the otherwise total darkness. We are left only with the sounds of frogs and goat-bells, and the single mournful strain of a flute...

Beside the near-dead body of RLS in his sleeping-bag there appears an old bear-hunter, JONATHAN WRIGHT, carrying a gun and muttering to himself.)

WRIGHT. God in heaven, what's this feller doin' ! Catching his death.

(WRIGHT picks up the prostrate RLS and carries him over his shoulder to the porch of a shack, now dimly outlined among the shadows at stage R. Setting RLS down gently, WRIGHT covers him, pours some whisky into him and sits beside him. HE sings softly in a rich bass voice, busying himself as he does so. The song is a cross between spiritual and lullaby.)

"LAY DOWN LOW" #17

LAY DOWN LOW,
LAY DOWN LOW,
SOMETHIN'S GONNA GETCHA
'LESS YA LAY DOWN LOW.

RABBIT IN THE BRUSH,
LOOKIN' FOR THE CORN,
LIST'NIN' CASE HE'LL NEVER SEE
THE NEX' DAY DAWN.
THEM AS RUNNIN' FAST,
THEM AS GOIN' SLOW,
COYOTE'S GONNA GETCHA
'LESS YA LAY DOWN LOW.

PHEASANTS ON THE WING,

FLAPPIN' ALL AROUND,
WATCHIN' OUT FOR TROUBLE
NEVER HEAR'D THE SOUND.
THEM AS RUNNIN' FAST,
THEM AS GOIN' SLOW,
THE COONS ARE GONNA GETCHA
'LESS YA LAY DOWN LOW.

GRIZZLY'S IN THE TREE,
THINKIN' HE'S FORGOT,
REACHIN' FOR THE HONEY
WHEN THE RIFLE SHOT.
THEM AS RUNNIN' FAST,
THEM AS GOIN' SLOW,
HUNTER'S GONNA GETCHA
'LESS YA LAY DOWN LOW.

LAY DOWN LOW,
LAY DOWN LOW,
VULTURES GONNA GETCHA
'LESS YA LAY DOWN LOW.

(By the end of the song, daylight has filtered over the shack. WRIGHT looks down again at the body beside him.)

WRIGHT. Reckon you and your Maker could take another whisky, eh, feller?

(HE reaches again for the bottle as the LIGHTS fade out.)

Scene 4

(The main street of Monterey. Weeks later, on market day. Outside the Bohemia Saloon - as for Scene 1 - the main street is crowded. A bright morning brings out the gossips and the traders. While the men hang around the swing-doors of the saloon, women gather into talkative pairs and groups. JONATHAN WRIGHT enters R, threading his way through the TOWNSFOLK. He doffs his hat to the women as HE passes, then stops for a few words with the horse-and-buggy DRIVER. While WRIGHT carries on his way and exits L, the DRIVER draws aside the FIRST TOWNSWOMAN and tells her what he's just heard. Within seconds wild rumours are spreading. The babble swells to a crescendo ...)

TOWNSFOLK. *(Overlapping phrases.)* It's that crackpot friend of Mrs. Osbourne's... Lawdy! They say for three days he went completely out of his mind! ... What would you expect - he's liter'y, ain't he?... Knew that one meant trouble... Sakes alive! Found him a-goner?... In San Clemente canyon - with all them bears up there! Is he dead then?... Eaten by a grizzly? My, oh, my!...

(FANNY enters down L, carrying a basket. Her brisk pace slows as, walking past the women, SHE catches an earful of their gossip.)

TOWNSFOLK. ...and her with that handsome husband and those sweet children... Well, it's the Lord's doing and I'm not surprised... Go on, you tell her!

(FANNY's interest has turned to anxiety. Out of the crowd the FIRST TOWNSWOMAN is pushed forward to break the news.)

1ST TOWNSWOMAN. Pardon me, Mrs. Osbourne, but we think you ought to know. Your - er - visiting lecturer er-hem... seems to have had an accident. They found him in the mountains. Quite, quite dead. So the rancher thought...

(In the shock of fear, FANNY drops her basket.)

1ST TOWNSWOMAN. But they do say he's not quite as dead as he was!

(The first TOWNSWOMAN fussily picks up FANNY's basket for her and rejoins the other women. The TOWNSFOLK disperse, still prattling, and exit in groups L and R. FANNY is left alone, overwrought, with tears of remembrance...)

Reprise: "NOT THIS MAN" #18

FANNY. *(Singing.)*
IF HE SHOULD STOP BREATHING!
SO SOON, SO UTTERLY!
THAT SILENCE, ENWREATHING,
STILL ACHING,
HEARTBREAKING -

WIN A PRIZE FOR CONSOLATION!
WHO WILL SHARE THE FIGHT,
DARING TO DEFY MY SHAME?
WHAT WOULD I GIVE TO WALK WITH PRIDE,
TO END THIS VAIN EMBROGLIO,
I'LL PAY MY PART!
TAKE ALL I OWE,
BUT NOT THIS MAN!
NO, NO, NO, NO,
NOT THIS MAN!

(As her song ends, WRIGHT re-enters L.   Seeing FANNY, he approaches her.)

WRIGHT. *(Doffing his hat.)* Pardon me, ma'am, I was looking for you. That Mr. Stevenson - your friend, I believe - what a time we've had with him! I don't know what rumours you've heard, but he was real sick at first. But oh boy, he's quite a character! *(HE laughs.)* I was kinda nursin' him up at the ranch, an' when he came round you know he jes' lay there an' spent a whole week tellin' my kids stories! Oh, he's right as rain again now, thank the Lord.

(FANNY, overjoyed, reaches out to WRIGHT and spontaneously hugs him.)

WRIGHT. *(Astonished.)* Well, thank you too, ma'am. *(HE smiles to himself and moves on, muttering.)* An' we sure could do with some rain... *(WRIGHT exits R.)*

(The musical coda of FANNY's song is heard as SHE paces to and fro. In evident excitement, SHE stops suddenly and gives a defiant shout.)

FANNY. To hell with them all! I want that divorce! *(SHE strides off R as the LIGHTS fade.)*

Scene 5

(Parlour of the Casa Bonifacio. That evening. The setting is as for Act II Scene 2. BELLE and NELLIE, clad in low-cut dancing dresses of red and yellow trimmed with black lace, are excited. While waiting for their beaux to take them to Monterey's weekly fandango, they tidy their appearance. NELLIE, with roses in her hair, tries to pin one into BELLE's. BELLE toys with her mantilla, feigning various attractive poses.)

NELLIE. You're wriggling again. Keep still, monkey!

BELLE. Lucky you to have a real fiancé! Joe's fun and I think he loves me, but whenever I mention you and Adolfo and getting married he just doesn't take the hint.

NELLIE. Getting married? *(SHE pauses glumly, sniffing a rose.)* Ever since our engagement Adolfo's been stuck at serenades. I sometimes wonder: if music be the food of love when do we reach the dessert?

BELLE. I don't think mama even likes Joe. And if she and papa are going to get a divorce, I'll be snubbed by everyone. It's hateful, Nellie! Oh, what would you do if you were me?

NELLIE. I would have a rose in my hair for tonight's fandango, and I'd stop wriggling.

(The sounds of guitar-strumming and clicking castanets are heard from outside, accompanying ADOLFO's now-familiar serenade.)

ADOLFO. *(Voice off, singing.)*
AY-AY-AY-AY,
NO ME DEJAS ASÍ, MI AMOR!
AY-AY-AY-AY -

BELLE AND NELLIE. *(Together.)* They're here already!

(As the girls adjust their décolletage, there is a loud knock at the door upcentre R. BELLE rushes to open it. ADOLFO and JOE spring into the room. Wearing fancy embroidered jackets and red sashes, the caballeros look 'dressed to kill'.)

ADOLFO. Cuantas chicas bonitas! *(HE kneels beside NELLIE, singing.)*
- UN BESO PARA MÍ, POR FAVOR!

(NELLIE playfully places a rose between his teeth. ADOLFO rises and pursues her round the room, begging for a kiss. JOE takes BELLE's hand while she strokes his embroidered jacket.)

JOE. *(To BELLE.)* Is your mother coming to the fandango? I hardly know how to behave without a chaperone.
BELLE. I don't know. She went to fetch Louis back from nowhere. How would I know what she wants?
JOE. Well I've decided I know what I want.
BELLE. Really, Joe? *(Softly, caressing his jacket.)* Will you tell me?

(JOE leans forward and kisses her. In another corner ADOLFO is winning his kiss from NELLIE. Suddenly the inside door L opens. LLOYD dashes in. The mood of romance is broken instantly.)

JOE. *(Crossly.)* If it's not mothers, it's little brothers!
LLOYD. Luly's back! Luly's back with mama, and he's been riding my pony!
ADOLFO. I knew it. Is a crackpot. *(HE strums a doleful chord.)*
LLOYD. And mama is laughing again. They're coming! See!

*(LLOYD runs to the outer door C, changes his mind, and
dashes off L. BELLE and NELLIE rush to a window
and peer out.)*

BELLE. Mama can't do this! *(In disgust, SHE flings
off her mantilla.)* Look, Nellie - she's bringing him
home arm-in-arm, in full view of everybody.
JOE. And about time too! *(HE drapes BELLE's
mantilla over a chair.)*
BELLE. No, Joe, I think it's awful. Why does she
have to look so happy?
JOE. Great. Don't you see - if she's happy how can
she say no about us?

*(LLOYD runs in again from L, now flourishing a
tambourine.)*

LLOYD. They're here. Come on, let's play the
entrance music!

*(ADOLFO starts up a paso doble on the guitar. JOE,
with castanets, and LLOYD, on tambourine, join in.
In the same party spirit BELLE and NELLIE show off
a few Spanish dancing steps. THEY make a colourful
tableau as the door as the door up R opens and RLS
and FANNY walk in together. RLS looks gaunt and
dishevelled as before but his spirits are now
unmistakably buoyant. His eyes light up at the sight
of the festive welcome "home".)*

RLS. Here's a stirring spectacle. The Act Four finale!
Missing only Monsieur Bizet's arpeggios and a chorus of

Andalusian olive-pickers. *(HE applauds the group, and addresses BELLE warmly.)* My, how pretty you look in your ringlets and ruffs... the silks of red and gold... that perfect rose... There's only one Belle of the ball!

BELLE. *(With a coy curtsy.)* Why, thank you, sir. *(Softening towards RLS at last.)* And welcome back to Monterey.

(RLS nods his appreciation, takes BELLE's hand and twirls her round him.)

FANNY. Now Louis, that was a long ride and I'm saddle-sore. All I ask is that you should be sensible.

RLS. Impeccably. I shall rest while you put on your operatic finery, and then we'll go.

FANNY. Go? Where?

RLS. To the fandango. Where else?

FANNY. Robert Louis Stevenson, you are out of your mind!

RLS. I was, yes. For some days, I'm told. But today, gladdened by that racing wind and this exotic company, I crave music and people, the thrill of a lilting melody! Adolfo understands.

(ADOLFO strikes a chord on the guitar to show his assent. LLOYD, as if prompted by a cue, suddenly dashes out through the inner door L.)

RLS. In short, Mrs. Osbourne, I wish to be your escort to the dance. I shall put on my gloves.

FANNY. This man is crazy! Louis Stevenson, you are a stupid, cantankerous maniac. You almost died up there, you know that? I will not go to the fandango, and nor will you.

RLS. *(Smiling, to BELLE.)* Your mother is a trifle peeved.

(LLOYD runs back in from the door at L, grinning. From behind his back HE produces a flageolet, RLS' own, and gives it to him.)

LLOYD. I bet this is what you wanted. I've been keeping it for you a whole year. Next to my box of beetles.

RLS. My pathetic little pipe! Thank you, Pettyfish. Does it still echo the skylark? *(HE plays a few hesitant notes, making FANNY smile and the others applaud.)* More like the nineteenth cuckoo in a belated spring.

(As RLS tries a few more notes on the flageolet, LLOYD makes a flourish with the tambourine. ADOLFO joins in on the guitar. JOE clicks his castanets. As THEY begin to make real music, LLOYD becomes very excited.)

LLOYD. Why can't we have our own fandango?

(With no further prompting BELLE and NELLIE execute some steps to the rhythm now led by ADOLFO. The musicians' efforts begin to take on a life of their own.)

FANNY. Absolutely not. No fandangos!

BEELE. Oh, why not, mama? Louis is back. We should celebrate.

FANNY. You go to the town fandango. Louis and I will take it easy.

BELLE. But he wants to go too. And he has to learn. Come on, Nellie! *(SHE coaxes NELLIE into a more elaborate routine while ADOLFO and JOE move alongside to accompany them.)*

FANNY. *(Thoroughly alarmed.)* I've told you, Belle. Louis can barely walk. Some day when he feels stronger ...

(But RLS too is defiant. HE tosses aside his flageolet and, with arms uplifted imperiously, calls out in mock-flamenco style as MUSIC begins...)

RLS. *(Sings.)*
FETCH ME A FANDANGO!

(All cheer except FANNY. THEY form a supportive circle around RLS as the orchestra picks up the MUSIC from his cue. FANNY protests to no avail.)

FANNY. No, Louis. This is ridiculous! Oh, won't anyone listen to me?

"FETCH ME A FANDANGO" #19

RLS.
FETCH ME A FANDANGO,
LET ME STRIKE A SPANISH POSE!
BRING THE BOLERO AND TANGO!

CABALLERO, TAP YOUR TOES!

SUMMON THE MUSICAL WAITERS,
CASTANETAS AND GUITAR!
SIGNAL THE IDLE SPECTATORS
TO CLAP WHERE THEY ARE!

FLOURISH SOMBRERO AND FAN! GO,
FIND A PARTNER, PARTISAN! GO
FETCH A FANDANGO!

(With BELLE as partner, HE essays a few flamenco-style moves which end in confusion and laughter. BELLE takes RLS aside to give him a lesson.)

BELLE.
I CAN SHOW HOW THEY DANCE 'LOS CAMOTES'
AND THE STEPS OF THE VARSOUVIANNA,
BUT THE VERY FIRST LESSON TO NOTE IS
HOW TO MOVE IN THE REQUISITE MANNER.
WITH THE HAND ON THE THIGH, AND THE TORSO
HELD AS STIFF AS A STATUE OR MORESO,
IT WON'T MATTER YOUR FOOTWORK IS SO-SO:
YOU COULD PASS AS A TRUE VIRTUOSO.
I KNOW SO.
   BELLE. *(Spoken.)* Come on, try again!
   BELLE. *(Singing.)*
TO-AND-FRO... SO!

(RLS tries again. This time the performance is more impressive. The onlookers shout support. Even FANNY's attitude begins to soften.)

RLS.
FETCH ME A FANDANGO!
ADIOS TO JIGS AND REELS!
BRING BACK THE BEAT WE BEGAN! GO,
SENORITA, CLICK YOUR HEELS!

(BELLE dances a short solo, then draws the others into the dance.)

BELLE.
MAKE IT A FAMILY FIESTA!
NO SIESTA! TAKE TO THE FLOOR!
RLS.
ENTER THE FRAY WITH THE ZEST OF
A CONQUISTADOR!

BELLE.
SING AS THE GYPSY FOLK SANG!
RLS.
IN AMERICAN SLANG,
LET THE WHOLE DAMN SHEBANG GO
IN A FANDANGO!

(The dance continues. Partners change - BELLE now with JOE, NELLIE with ADOLFO. LLOYD finally coaxes FANNY onto the floor to partner RLS. The others back away to leave RLS and FANNY dancing together in centre stage.)

ALL. *(Reprise.)*
MAKE IT A FAMILY FIESTA!
NO SIESTA! TAKE TO THE FLOOR!
  MEN.
ENTER THE FRAY WITH THE ZEST OF
A CONQUISTADOR!
  ALL.
SING AS THE GYPSY FOLK SANG!
IN AMERICAN SLANG,
LET THE WHOLE DAMN SHEBANG GO
IN A FANDANGO! OLÉ!

(When the song ends, in a tableau, BELLE, JOE, NELLIE, and ADOLFO make their exit through the door upcentre R. RLS and FANNY sink onto the sofa.)

RLS. Phew! It's a hot night in the Casa Bonifacio.

FANNY. You look like a toasted tumbleweed.

RLS. The air outside would cool our soles. Madam, will you walk?

LLOYD. I will, Luly. Come! *(HE tries to draw RLS up off the sofa.)*

RLS. Gladly, if I have permission.

LLOYD. Look! After all that fuss, Belle's forgotten her mantilla. *(HE indicates the black shawl draped over a chair.)*

FANNY. That reminds me, Louis, we must talk about that young lady. Lloyd, dear, would you please wait for Luly outside?

(LLOYD picks up RLS' flageolet, trying to play it as HE exits L.)

FANNY. It's about Belle and Joe.
RLS. Young love has caught their fancy. It makes a pretty picture.

(Unseen, JOE re-enters up C, looking for BELLE's mislaid mantilla.)

FANNY. The trouble with Joe is he's got talent but no prospects. Belle has quite a few admirers. I may even have found her an ideal husband.

(JOE listens, alarmed. HE grabs the mantilla and exits, up C, in haste.)

RLS. More of your sorcery? Fanny, please! *(HE rises.)* Marriages, my doctor tells me, are best swallowed one at a time.
FANNY. Yes, my love, but it costs plenty to keep a family. We can't expect Sam -
RLS. I don't. I'm not afraid to work harder. *(HE draws FANNY up into a tender embrace, kissing her gently.)* Lloyd must be waiting for me.

(The LIGHTS are dimming as RLS moves quietly away from FANNY and exits in search of LLOYD.)

FANNY. *(Ruminating, to herself.)* No, my darling, you're never afraid... But I am.

(The LIGHT on FANNY fades out.)

Scene 6

(The shores of Monterey. Late evening. In faint moonlight blurred by the evening fog of the shoreline RLS appears, moving briskly and closely followed by LLOYD. THEY are tramping through woods and sandhills, accompanied by the sounds of screaming seagulls and the thundering surge of the Pacific surf.)

LLOYD. Please, Luly, you walk too fast. My feet are aching. If only my legs were longer... *(HE stops and sinks to the ground.)*

RLS. You could stride above the forest with your head among the stars. *(Alert and eager, HE moves restlessly in the evocative atmosphere.)* Do you hear the ocean rumbling? The voices in the wind? Quick, the buccaneers are on our trail! Bury the treasure, young master, and run for the thicket. I see the gleam of a swinging cutlass now. Look there, a dozen of them! Muttering foul curses, swearing their bloodthirsty vengeance, and we as loyal a crew as ever ploughed the seven seas under the King's flag!

LLOYD. I can't bury the treasure, Luly. You still have it.

RLS. *(Stopping suddenly, the illusion broken, HE looks glumly at the flageolet in his hand.)* Lord help me, matey, I thought this was a musket.

LLOYD. *(Tired and preoccupied.)* Luly, please tell me what happened at the bear-hunter's shack. You had real fever. Mama said you were dying.

RLS. I was ill. *(HE leans on a tree beside him, reflective.)* I even wrote my epitaph. But as you see, I didn't die.

LLOYD. Not then. But you're not really well again, are you?

RLS. Perhaps not. I do seem to accumulate illnesses. But with as few doubloons as I have I must keep on writing, mustn't I?

LLOYD. You look thin. You always look thin. If I found real treasure, like a casket of gold pieces, would you eat more often?

RLS. At Simoneau's restaurant I can enjoy a banquet every day.   Monsieur Simoneau is the best cook in California, with the single exception of your mother. Besides, laddie, this discussion is too morbid. I prefer our adventure stories.

LLOYD. So do I. But if you die, there won't be any more, anyway.

RLS. *(Striding about impatiently.)* This is nonsense, laddie. You sound as melancholy as my father, waiting for Divine Providence to pull out the pocket-watch. There's more fun to be enjoyed than that, young master. Think of the stories, the dangers we have to dodge... the amazing people we meet! The lightkeeper, playing his piano in that solitary tower. The Portuguese whalers - or were they swashbuckling pirates? That's enough gloom, young Mr. Osbourne, sir, we haven't finished our adventures yet!

(The rhythm of the plunging surf cues the MUSIC of his song.)

"IF I LIVE" #20

RLS. *(Sings.)*
I'LL NEVER BUILD A LIGHTHOUSE
NOR PLEAD IN COURTS OF LAW,
BUT DESTINY
IS TELLING ME
WHAT MY BRIEF TIME IS FOR.

IF I LIVE
WE'LL SAIL OUR VESSEL TO EXOTIC LANDS,
IMAGINE CHARACTERS ON SILVER SANDS
AND LET THEM TRAP US IN THEIR SNARE;
THEN WATCH THE DRAMA OF THEIR LIVES
    UNFOLD.
WE'LL HEAR THEIR STORIES TOLD -
SO MANY FRIENDS TO SHARE
IF I LIVE.

IF I LIVE
WE'LL TAKE A FOOTPATH INTO MYSTERY,
THROUGH SILENT PASSAGES OF HISTORY
WHERE FELLOW-DREAMERS STAYED AWHILE,
WE'LL MAKE ACQUAINTANCE WITH THE
    THINGS THEY'VE DONE,
THEIR BATTLES LOST AND WON,
AND TELL THEIR TALES WITH STYLE
IF I LIVE.

LOOK OUT FOR CREEPING SHADOWS!
STAY STILL! WHY THE RUSH TO HIDE?
TAKE COURAGE FROM REALITY:
THERE GOES YOUR DARKER SIDE.

IF I LIVE
WE'LL COMB THE HEATHER OF MY NATIVE
  HILLS.
WITH CUNNING WORDS AND UNEXPECTED
  SKILLS
WE'LL FIGHT FOR JUSTICE OR TO DIE.
AND TREASURE-HUNTERS ON AN ISLAND
  SHORE
WILL FIND ONE STORY MORE -
THAT GOLD I HAVE TO GIVE
IF I LIVE... IF I LIVE.

*(LLOYD is still sitting, hands clasping knees, his
attention riveted throughout the song. When it ends
RLS helps LLOYD to his feet.)*

RLS. *(Spoken.)* I want to tell you something. You
may not like it, but I hope you will. I am going to marry
your mother.

*(LLOYD is dumbstruck with joy, puts his hand into
LULY's and looks up at him fondly. Together, in
fading LIGHT, they start the long walk home.)*

Scene 7

(Letters between Edinburgh, London, and Monterey. The settings are identified by spotlight and character. CHARLES BAXTER, sitting alone at his desk in Edinburgh with a half-empty whisky bottle in front of him, is the focal point of a dialogue by correspondence in which RLS, THOMAS, and COLVIN are the other participants.   As RLS' designated "post-office" BAXTER is seen handling a stream of letters, from and to RLS, most of which are arriving only after many weeks delay.   SPOTLIGHTS illuminate in turn the several correspondents in their respective locations: RLS in Monterey, COLVIN in London with MRS. SITWELL beside him, and THOMAS with MARGARET STEVENSON at home, like BAXTER, in Edinburgh.   BAXTER handles the business with his usual cheerful stoicism.)

BAXTER. *(Reading a letter from RLS.)* "My dear Charles... I passed the salt sea with comparative impunity, having only lost a stone... Am now quite the accomplished emigrant. I keep in truly wonderful spirits, all things considered. Address me care of Joe Strong, Monterey, California. When you write you must give me news of my parents..."

THOMAS. *(Talking to MARGARET.)* Never a word from him. The man's a nomad. Wasting his life and ruining ours, all this for this witch of a woman.

BAXTER. *(Reading letter from RLS.)* "My dear Charles... This is not a letter, for I am too perturbed. I am still thirty pounds to the good. You had better send me fifty of my precious hundred. You may say where I am. But remember... my address is to be given to no one, not even the Queen."

THOMAS. *(Talking to MARGARET.)* If we only knew where to write. He sends no address. Nothing. It's as if he'd vanished off the face of the earth.

BAXTER. *(Reading, from RLS.)* "I write to you from an Angora goat ranch where I live with an old bear-hunter... Times and seasons are quite beyond me now. I am pretty well dished. But tell me, please, Charles, for God's sake, how about my father?"

THOMAS. *(To MARGARET, reading a letter from BAXTER.)* Aye, he's found a fine pit of iniquity now. Baxter says he's in California! If that's not the end of the world...

RLS. *(Reading, from BAXTER.)* "My dear Louis... I was glad to have your letter of the 9th. I should be glad to have another, a little more intelligible. I send £ 50 as requested..."

BAXTER. *(Reading, from RLS.)* "Perhaps you will send the £ 50 I asked for in my last. Things are damned complicated. You may spare my people the tidings. But tell Colvin..."

COLVIN. *(Talking to MRS. SITWELL.)* "Complicated"... and quite unnecessary. Our wanderer is a wreck. The mail is absurdly slow. The editors begin to despair of him. Where does he think Mrs. O is leading him?

RLS. *(Writing to COLVIN.)* I am in good health now. I work at the notes of my voyage. My book is half-drafted: the "Amateur Emigrant", that is...

COLVIN. *(Reading from RLS' letter.)* "I believe it will be more popular than the others" ! Pah! Come back soon, he must. What disturbs me most of all is that the works he has sent me are not good. I doubt whether they are saleable. If his work is no good how is he to live?

BAXTER. *(Reading from RLS.)* " ...and my father, Charles?"

THOMAS. *(Writing to COLVIN.)* Our case is painful beyond expression. For God's sake use your influence...

COLVIN. *(Reading from THOMAS' letter.)* " ... your influence. Is it fair that we should be half-murdered by his conduct?"

RLS. *(Writing to BAXTER.)* Since I have gone away I have found out for the first time how much I love that man...

THOMAS. *(Writing to COLVIN.)* I see nothing but destruction to himself and to all of us.

RLS. *(Writing to BAXTER.)* I wish they would cheer up. In coming here I did the right thing. The effect of my arrival has been...

BAXTER. *(Reading from RLS' letter.)* " ...has been to straighten out everything."

THOMAS. *(To BAXTER.)* He should come back at once. Aye, ye can tell him his father's ill and that's the truth of it.

RLS. *(Reading, from BAXTER.)* "My dear Louis, please acknowledge receipt." *(Exasperated, HE writes back to BAXTER.)* Dear Charles, I will not desert my wife!

BAXTER. *(Reading from RLS.)* "There is to be a private divorce in January and yours truly will be a married man as soon thereafter as decency and the law permit..."

THOMAS. Dear God!

COLVIN. Dear me!

BAXTER. *(Reading a postscript from RLS.)* " ...the only question is whether I shall be alive for the ceremony."

(SPOTLIGHTS fade from all but BAXTER, who stands and gulps down the remains of his whisky-bottle.)

BAXTER. 'Struth! It's enough to drive a man to drink!

(The SPOTLIGHT on BAXTER also fades out.)

Scene 8

(Simoneau's Restaurant, Monterey. The scene is the interior of the grubby restaurant run by JULES SIMONEAU, a benign, bearded expatriate Frenchman in his late fifties. The street entrance, upcentre L, is flanked by murals on the walls. At one side there is a long, cloth-covered dining-table. At

the other, with a carafe and glass of wine before him, RLS sits at a small side-table littered with manuscripts, notebooks, and letters. HE is flipping envelopes over his shoulder, with mounting frustration. SIMONEAU stands by, wiping plates, listening to RLS. It is early evening.)

RLS. Editors! They toss me balloons, bursting with gaseous promises. Ah, mon ami, Old Europe frowns upon its exiles. Picture the editorial counting-house, the cosy clubroom, the assembled caffeine-sippers in their lair. Squatting on their hams and nodding like dyspeptic mandarins.   They sniff my work and reach for the scolding quill... *(In a mocking voice.)* "If it were only consistent... if only you would come back to us"! What petty, futile fantasies. It's here the play is on the stage, not in their gallery.

SIMONEAU. You haven't eaten for three days.

RLS. So many?

SIMONEAU. Ten years from now, they'll lick your boots. But not if the boots are empty. Tiens, mon cher, put some wisdom in your stomach!

RLS. Thanks to you, my friend, I enjoy two virtues - your wine and my discipline. You know we slingers of ink must earn our daily baguette. *(HE resumes writing.)* Today, I am earning. Tomorrow, the baguette!

SIMONEAU. Today bouillabaisse. It's on the house.

RLS. The aroma is enticing. Chalk it up to my account or else the auld alliance is in tatters.

SIMONEAU. Stubborn Scot!

RLS. Gentil Gaulois! You're the kindest man I know.

(A Spanish-speaking DINER enters and cheerily hails RLS.)

1ST DINER. Hola, Don Louis! You write us all another story?
    RLS. Hola, amigo! I think I'm scalping windmills.
    1ST DINER. I doan unnerstan. Windmills?
    RLS. Forgive me. I talk no sense today.

(The FIRST DINER prepares to take his place at the dining-table, which SIMONEAU is nonchalantly setting. A SECOND DINER (Italian) enters from the street and hails RLS.)

2ND DINER. Buon giorno, Don Louis. Howza novella?
    RLS. Buon giorno, amigo. Not good. Howza fishing these days?

(As other DINERS come in, they all hail RLS like an old friend, and a cosmopolitan spirit of bonhomie prevails as they assemble. RLS struggles to write while waving back to acknowledge each greeting and fending off hand-shakes. The noise mounts. Last but not least, ADOLFO enters. Seeing RLS and hearing the babble, ADOLFO reaches into his holster, pulls out his pistol and - as in II.1 - fires it in the air. All jump, and there is instant silence.)

ADOLFO. I tole you before. You doan in'errupt Don Louis while he write a beautiful story, okay? Hola, Louis!

RLS. Hola, Adolfo! Today, it's the "Emigrant" who plagues me. I should throw him in the melting-pot.

(ADOLFO joins the other DINERS assembling round the long dining-table. SIMONEAU moves among them. While pretending a clatter of plates and cutlery, HE draws them into a whispered conspiracy, carried out in dumbshow with furtive glances and gesticulations towards RLS. RLS, busy at his manuscript, sees nothing.)

SIMONEAU. *(Bluntly, in a loud whisper to the* conspirators.*)* The guy's sick an' the guy's broke. So that's what we do. Okay?

(The DINERS makes noises of agreement. The huddle resumes. SIMONEAU produces a newspaper and makes play with it while the others look to RLS and instinctively pat their pockets.)

ADOLFO. *(To SIMONEAU.)* Is a deal. Okay.

(SIMONEAU nods with satisfaction. Newspaper in hand, HE crosses to RLS.)

SIMONEAU. *(To RLS.)* Have you seen this?
RLS. *(Looking up.)* The Monterey Californian. Our spyglass on the universe. Not exactly a mine of information on the cataclysmic events of our time. *(Taking SIMONEAU's copy and looking it over.)* Where may I read here of the scientific revolution? the exultant march of electricity? or Mr. Bell's intriguing new device,

the telephone? Ah-h-h! *(His attention is caught by a front page item.)* Mrs. Jones bought a box of hairpins yesterday. Whereas I see Mrs. Potter is investing in purple petticoats!

SIMONEAU. You've been offered a job as part-time reporter at two dollars a week. Take it or leave it.

RLS. *(Sounding shocked.)* Writing for the local rag?! Now that would confound my friend Colvin and his pards!

(The DINERS drift towards RLS, flourishing more copies of the newspaper.)

1ST DINER. Why not, Don Louis? Everybody reads it around here.

2ND DINER. Circulates for miles. There's even a subscriber in San Francisco.

3RD DINER. So you break into the great American market!

ADOLFO. Do us a favour, Louis. Is good for Bohemia business. Everyone wanna read what you write.

SIMONEAU. You hear what they say? What about it?...

"LOCAL RAG" #21

(MUSIC begins: initially a quiet and fairly free accompaniment to the introduction, which is spoken as much as sung by SIMONEAU and RLS.)

SIMONEAU. Let your contributions add style to our chronicle.

RLS.   I wonder... flipping over the pages I find it ironical.
THAT HERE'S A PAPER,
A LOCAL WEEKLY PAPER,
SUDDENLY AROUSING AN ACUTE NOSTALGIA.
NAMES MY PLAYFUL FANCY FILES AWAY
LEAP TO LIFE SIX THOUSAND MILES AWAY.
IT STIRS THE EMBERS,
AFFECTIONS ONE REMEMBERS,
THE TRIVIA OF DELIGHTFUL CONVERSATIONS.
THE FRIEND IN NEED
HAS A FRIEND INDEED
HERE IN THE LOCAL RAG.
    SIMONEAU. So you'll take the job?
    RLS. How can I resist the purple petticoats?
    SIMONEAU. You do us a great honour, Mon Cher. Tomorrow - the baguette!

(SIMONEAU shakes RLS' hand warmly. Behind him the diners show noisy approval. Unseen by RLS, ADOLFO whips his hat round the others and each drops in a quarter coin. The MUSIC swings into neo-ragtime rhythm.)

    ADOLFO. Now is gonna be a great newspaper. Best in California!
    SIMONEAU. *(Singing.)*
IT'S IN THE PAPER,
IN THE LOCAL PAPER,
ALL YOU NEED TO KNOW ABOUT YOUR NEXT-
    DOOR NEIGHBOURS.

1ST DINER.
LEARN HOW HENRY CAUGHT HIS FLORA
   2ND DINER.
POURING ON THE HAIR-RESTORER.
   ADOLFO.
LUCY DICKENS
LOST A PAIR O' CHICKENS,
   3RD DINER.
PEGGED 'EM ON THE WASHING-LINE MONDAY.
   SIMONEAU.
THERE'S   GOOD   NEWS   FOR   OUR   FRIEND
   SYDNEY.
   ADOLFO.
DOC JUST FOUND THAT MISSING KIDNEY.
   ALL.
OUR TOWN FOLK ALL
READ THE LOCAL RAG.

   ADOLFO.
IS IN THE PAPER,
STARING IN THE PAPER,
EVERYTHING YOU PEEPING AT BEHIND LACE
   CURTAINS.
   4TH DINER.
READ HOW CHARLIE'S MARE IS FARING.
   5TH DINER.
LOOK UP WHAT HIS WIFE IS WEARING.
   RLS.
POOR PEPITA,
MARRIED TO A CHEATER,
KNITTING UP IN BED SHE GETS STITCHES,

SIMONEAU.
A GREAT BREAK FOR RAUNCHY READERS:
STEVE'S IN TOWN AND BROUGHT HIS
BREEDERS.
   ALL.
RANCHER FOLK ALL
READ THE LOCAL RAG.

   RLS.
SPORTING COLUMNS BOAST THEIR BREVITY.
   DINERS.
LYNCHING'S IN AND SHOOTING'S OUT.
   RLS.
BUSINESS IN RECESSION, SEE PAGE TWO.
FASHION NOTES SHOW MORE LONGEVITY,
CORSETS STILL INCLINE TO LEVITY.
   ALL.
WHY?
   RLS.
IT'S ANOTHER OF NATURE'S WONDERS.

   SIMONEAU AND ADOLFO. *(Together.)*
THEY'RE IN THE PAPER,
LEAKING THROUGH THE PAPER,
ALL THE JUICY BUNCHES OFF THE BACKYARD
   GRAPEVINE:
   1ST DINER.
ELMER'S GUEST IS DATING DUSTY,
   2ND DINER.
SAYS OLD ELMER'S SPRINGS GOT RUSTY.
   DINERS.
KEEP IT QUIET,

LOLA'S ON A DIET,
CUTTIN' DOWN HER RESIDENT BOARDERS.
RLS.
WELL, HATS OFF TO IDA HACKETT -
SLUGGED HER JACK AND PAWNED HIS JACKET!
  ALL.
SMARTER FOLK'LL
READ THE LOCAL RAG.
MAKE YOUR MIND UP: WHICH IS DULLER -
PLAIN TRUTH OR LOCAL COLOUR?
HONEST FOLK ALL
READ THE LOCAL RAG.

*(Time permitting, this can be a false ending followed by
  more stories:)*

  ALL.
IT'S IN THE PAPER,
SIZZLING IN THE PAPER.
WHAT YOU MAY HAVE MISSED ABOUT THAT
  **** IN SCARLET:

  RLS.
SLEEPLESS NIGHTS FOR OUR REPORTER,
BORN TO ROSIE HUGHES, A DAUGHTER.
  ADOLFO.
SPOT THE WINNER!
  SIMONEAU.
"WANTED, A BEGINNER -
MUSTN'T BE ALLERGIC TO GRANDMA"
  RLS.
AND WHAT'S THIS? A JAILHOUSE JOKER?

"SHERIFF STRIPPED WHILE PLAYING POKER"
  ALL.
KEEP HIM COVERED
WITH THE LOCAL RAG!

  RLS.
HERE'S AN ITEM, SURELY SPURIOUS:
"ANACONDA STRIKES AGAIN! -
TAXIDERMIST STUFFED BY WILY PET"
CIRCUMSTANCES RATHER CURIOUS,
WIFE CONFESSES SHE WAS FURIOUS.
  ALL.
WHY?
  RLS.
SHE'D HAVE DONE IT WITH SAGE AND ONION.

  ALL.
THEY FILL THE PAPER,
SCOOP IT FOR THE PAPER,
EVERY LOAD OF BULLSHIT
DROPPED IN MAIN STREET DOORWAYS.
  SIMONEAU.
BOSS SHOULD LET THE HOT STUFF COOL A BIT.
  ALL.
UNDERTAKER'S HEARSE IS FULL OF IT.
  RLS.
THE CHURCH IS LIVID:
WHY MAKE LIFE SO VIVID?
JUDGMENT DAY IS COMING, BE PREPARED,
  LADS!
  A DINER.
"PARSON FAVOURS STERN POSITION"

ALL.
HOLD IT - TILL THE NEXT EDITION!
COME AND JOIN US, WAVE THE LOCAL FLAG.
EVERYBODY READ THE LOCAL RAG!

(The song and dance end in a tableau.)

SIMONEAU. And now, amigos, la bouillabaisse!

(Before THEY can sit LLOYD rushes in, looking around frantically.)

LLOYD. Luly! Adolfo! I knew I'd find you here. You must come - quickly. Something's happened.
ADOLFO. What is?
LLOYD. It's Belle and Joe. They've gone to San Francisco and gotten married. And mama and Aunt Nellie are going to find them. You must come!
ADOLFO. Ay-ay-ay-ay!
RLS. Oh, no, not more complications...
SIMONEAU. Courage, mon cher! Sounds like you got your first news story.

(LLOYD rushes out again, followed by ADOLFO. RLS hastily gathers up his manuscript and letters, feels in his pocket for a few coins, and staggers towards the door.)

RLS. One Osbourne family... plus five cats, two dogs and three horses! Yes, they make a story.

(As RLS exits in a hurry, the LIGHTS fade out.)

Scene 9

(Apartments in San Francisco. The scene represents a triptych of separate apartments in different locations across the city - simple rooms, each with a door, lit in turn as the action moves from one to the other. From downstage L, FANNY strides into the foreground with NELLIE trailing in her wake. THEY are accompanied by the bounding introductory MUSIC for the song which follows. FANNY makes for stage R, where she pushes open the door of the first apartment. BELLE and JOE are suddenly illuminated; THEY are clearly on the defensive. FANNY confronts them, hands on hips, with a combative stare directed at JOE.)

JOE. I didn't steal her. I swear I'm going to make her a very happy woman.
FANNY. I've heard that one before!

"THE BEST OF INTENTIONS" #22

FANNY. *(Singing.)*
YOU MARRIED, YOU SAY, WITH THE BEST OF
    INTENTIONS,
THE BEST OF INTENTIONS, NOW WHAT DOES
    THAT MEAN?
UNLESS I'M DELUDED BY MISAPPREHENSIONS

YOUR BEST OF INTENTIONS ARE NOT WORTH A
  BEAN!

GET WORK, BY MONDAY AT FOUR!
ELSE YOU'LL GET HELL FROM YOUR MOTHER-
  IN-LAW!
  NELLIE. *(Echoing her.)*
TRA-LA-LA-LA: MONDAY AT FOUR!
TRA-LA-LA-LA-LA: OR TROUBLE IN STORE.
  FANNY.
THE PARTY IS OVER, DON'T ASK FOR
  EXTENSIONS.
IT'S TIME YOU CONFESSED YOUR INTENTIONS!

*(FANNY slams the door on JOE and BELLE. With
NELLIE still in tow she strides on to the second
apartment. There it is husband SAM who is now
illuminated. HE too is on the defensive as FANNY
storms through the door.)*

SAM. It's a slow business, but I'll go see what my
lawyer can do. I give you my word.
  FANNY. Your word is a dead duck!

  FANNY. *(Singing.)*
YOU SWORE TO DIVORCE WITH THE BEST OF
  INTENTIONS,
THE BEST OF INTENTIONS, THE IFS AND THE
  BUTS.
I'M SICK TO THE TEETH WITH YOUR CUTE
  CIRCUMVENTIONS,

THE TEST OF INTENTIONS IS HAVING THE
    GUTS!

I'LL BE HERE TUESDAY AT NINE.
GET OUT THE DOCUMENTS READY TO SIGN!
    NELLIE. *(Echoing.)*
TRA-LA-LA-LA: TUESDAY AT NINE.
TRA-LA-LA-LA-LA-LA: SIGN ON THE LINE!
    FANNY.
THE PARTY IS OVER, DON'T ASK FOR
    EXTENSIONS.
IT'S TIME I UNDRESSED YOUR INTENTIONS.

*(SHE slams the door on SAM, and simultaneously the
    LIGHT on him goes out. While FANNY strides on,
    NELLIE meditates.)*

    NELLIE. Me too. *(Sighing.)* Oh, Adolfo!
    NELLIE. *(Singing.)*
BETROTHAL, HE SAID, SHOWS THE BEST OF
    INTENTIONS.
THE REST OF INTENTIONS ARE FADING AWAY.
MY   DARLING   FIANCÉ,   FORGET   THE
    CONVENTIONS,
THE TEST OF INTENTIONS IS NAMING THE DAY!

NOT ONE MORE SWEET SERENADE.
ALL I WANT NOW IS A WEDDING PARADE.

*(FANNY and NELLIE meet again in centre stage. THEY
    stand together, uncompromising.)*

FANNY AND NELLIE. *(Singing together.)*
MEN, MEN DON'T BE AFRAID!
STAND AND DELIVER THE PROMISES YOU
    MADE!
THE PARTY IS OVER, DON'T ASK FOR
    EXTENSIONS
SO BEST MANIFEST YOUR INTENTIONS!

(THEY whirl back to the first apartment, at far R, to confront JOE and BELLE a second time. This time JOE is elated)

JOE. Good news. A commission from a sugar baron. He wants me to paint Hawaii!
    FANNY. Now that's what I like to hear!

(BELLE and NELLIE embrace. FANNY gives JOE a discreet peck. The LIGHT goes out on the newlyweds. FANNY and NELLIE return to confront SAM again in the second, central, apartment.)

SAM. Whaddyaknow? These lawyers can really move when they want to. *(HE hands the divorce documents to FANNY.)*
    FANNY. You son of a gun! See you in court, Sam!

(FANNY and NELLIE hug each other in celebration, and the LIGHT goes out on SAM. While MUSIC continues, NELLIE exits R. FANNY exits L, passing the third apartment. MUSIC slows and softens as this room is gradually illuminated. Inside RLS, in black velvet jacket, is seen on a couch with a writing-pad on

his knee. HE starts coughing and hastily covers his mouth with a handkerchief. HE is staring desperately at a crimson stain on the handkerchief when FANNY bursts into the room through an inner sidedoor up L.)

FANNY. Louis, love! The divorce is settled, we can

(SHE breaks off, rushes to the couch, and removes her own coat to wrap around RLS. With her arms round his shoulders, SHE tries to warm and comfort him simultaneously. The MUSIC is fading out.)

RLS. I hardly know what's left to me, Fanny. Pleurisy, malaria, now this. The good doctor declares I have consumption. I am all in a chitter again. How can I work like this? Why can't I just go and be done?

(FANNY produces a sedative and gives it to RLS.)

RLS. What's this? *(HE looks dejectedly at the pill.)* Another dice to roll at my friend? We have been playing this game so long now, the rogue should have sought a more amenable partner.

FANNY. *(Calmly soothing.)* Enough, Louis. I'm here. We'll be together now, and I'll not let you go.

RLS. If I could only work! I have yet to pay my board and lodging to humanity. I write nothing of value - except letters. I managed one to Baxter and this to Colvin... *(HE passes it to her.)* A little short on humour. As for my "Emigrant", poor fellow...

FANNY. *(Studying the letter.)* This inky oblong - "A sketch of my tomb", you say. Huh! *(SHE reads on,* *quoting.)* "Home is the sailor, home from sea,/And the hunter home from the hill." And you're sending that to Colvin! Louis, I won't have it like this. When did Colvin last write to you? Have the lousy editors sent you what they owe? And your parents...

(RLS, weak and weary, appears to be falling asleep.)

FANNY. Have you told them anything? Or do you leave that to Charlie Baxter? Do they know how sick you really are?

(The MUSIC of her song is heard again as FANNY tries to control her emotion. SHE sings haltingly, and more slowly than before.)

FANNY. *(Singing.)*
THEY WORRY AND WAIL WITH THE BEST OF
    INTENTIONS,
PROTEST THEIR INTENTIONS ON EVERY
    FLANK.
THERE'S ONLY ONE ITEM THAT NOBODY
    MENTIONS:
THE TEST OF INTENTIONS IS BUCKS IN THE
    BANK.

(Resolutely, FANNY picks up pen and paper, and starts a letter.)

PLEASE, PLEASE, IT'S TIME YOU FORGAVE!
THIS IS THE FACE WE ARE WANTING TO SAVE!

(The MUSIC stops abruptly, and the scene BLACKS OUT.)

Scene 10

(Thomas Stevenson's study. The setting is as for Act I, Scenes 3 & 10. A rare bright winter morning brings sunlight through the window. CHARLES BAXTER, the messenger, stands between THOMAS and MARGARET STEVENSON, characteristically trying to put a cheerful face on a sombre scene.)

BAXTER. Please forward this letter to my mother, he says. *(HE hands MARGARET an envelope.)* And please convey to my father, he says, my fondest hope that he will assist the disposal of - I quote - "my library".

THOMAS. *(Aghast.)* His books? He wants me to sell off his books?!

MARGARET. *(Opening the envelope.)*   How strange. It's not his handwriting.

BAXTER. He says he wishes he could keep them all, but ad interim, a pound or two would help.

THOMAS. Aye, so he's become a penniless tramp. Well it's his own sinful doing.

MARGARET. *(While reading.)* Och, Tom, he's in danger of... *(SHE reads on, in tears.)*

THOMAS. *(To BAXTER.)* And he talks seriously of marrying this divorcee? That's where he's been putting his pittance. Keeping the woman.

BAXTER. No, I don't think we could argue post hoc ergo propter hoc, as it were. Under American law the husband is obliged to maintain the wife and family through all proceedings until the divorce is final.

THOMAS. And is it? *(Impatient as BAXTER shrugs.)* Well, has he?

BAXTER. *(Shrugs again.)* In such a situation my client - excuse me! Louis - is, as you know, temperamentally inclined towards generosity.

MARGARET. *(Finishes reading, wiping away tears.)* Well, she does write a bonny letter, I'll say that for her.

THOMAS. It's from herself?

MARGARET. *(Quoting.)* "With understanding and affection, Fanny Vandegrift Osbourne". Och, she sounds a truly caring woman, nursing him night and day for his lungs, the puir lad... that terrible consumption...

THOMAS. The consumption again, ye say?

MARGARET. And it's bad this time. Aye, she's a caring woman - even if she is divorced.

THOMAS. What's that got to do with it?

MARGARET. Now, Tom! After all these months of you on your high horse!

THOMAS. What high horse? You know my views on divorce well enough, my dear. A woman should have a divorce whenever she wants, but a man never!

(BAXTER smiles, surprised and encouraged by signs of changing attitudes.)

BAXTER. In my opinion it's in such circumstances as these that the offended parties might consider... er...

making allowances. *(HE pauses for effect.)* In favour of the... er... party of the first part, as it were... or, viewed from the perspective of this family home, the party of the second part...

THOMAS. I don't quite follow your gist. An' what's a lawyer doing in all this, anyway?

BAXTER. As the party of the third part, I'd say... for heaven's sake, he loves her and he wants to marry her!

THOMAS. *(Mulling it over.)* Aye, well he's waited long enough to be respectable.

BAXTER. Think of it, Mr. Stevenson, ye'd no be losing a son, ye'd be gaining the United States.

THOMAS. Aye, well I never was an empire man meself.

BAXTER. Hang it, Louis has eaten enough humble pie! Ye've got a genius for a son, and he's broke. Can ye no put that in your theology?!

"MAKING ALLOWANCES" #23

BAXTER. *(Singing.)*
PITY THE WRETCHED SOUL,
TORN FROM HIS NEXT OF KIN,
SUNK IN THE DEEPEST HOLE,
UP TO HIS NECK IN SIN.
THERE GOES YOUR ONLY SON!
MY FRIEND FROM EARLY TEENS!
SO MANY YEARS OF FUN,
TO END WITHOUT THE MEANS!
   THOMAS.
ALL WE CAN DO IS PRAY.

BAXTER.
A CHRISTIAN MAN COULD SAY...

JESUS SAVES BY MAKING ALLOWANCES,
DIPPING IN A POCKET FOR THE POOR AND
    NEEDY,
TAKE THIS TEXT FOR MAKING ALLOWANCES:
CHARITY BEGINS AT HOME
SWEET HOME.

*(MARGARET moves to stand with BAXTER in winning
    over her husband.)*

MARGARET.
I'M FOR ENGINEERING ALLOWANCES,
OPENING A BRIDGE TO THE INFIRM AND
    LONELY.
STAKE THAT PILE ON MAKING ALLOWANCES.
CHARITY BEGINS AT HOME
SWEET HOME.

*(THOMAS starts pacing up and down. HE is beginning
    to waver.)*

BAXTER.
BLESSED THE MAN WHO ACTS!
MARGARET.
BLESSED BE THE TRULY QUICK!
THOMAS.
IF WE COULD KNOW THE FACTS...
BAXTER.
FIGURES WILL DO THE TRICK.

MARGARET.
THINK OF THE PLEASURES PAST!
BAXTER.
THINK OF THE FAME TO COME!
THOMAS. *(Spoken.)* Mebbe a loan ...?
BAXTER and MARGARET. *(Singing together.)*
AT LAST!
BAXTER.
A DECENT, RESPECTABLE SUM?!

(THOMAS pulls out his pocketbook, writes down a figure and shows it to BAXTER.)

THOMAS. *(Spoken.)* What d'ye think he'd say to that?
BAXTER. *(Spoken.)* He just might faint away.
ALL. *(Singing.)*
JESUS SAVES BY MAKING ALLOWANCES
THOMAS and MARGARET. *(Together.)*
WELCOMING THE PRODIGAL
BAXTER.
WITH MORE THAN OATCAKES
ALL.
 ENGINEERING FAMILY ALLOWANCES:
CHARITY BEGINS AT HOME
SWEET HOME!

(Tableau and BLACKOUT.)

Scene 11

(Fanny's Cottage, Oakland, 1880. Weeks have passed. In the cottage drawing-room RLS, with a writing-pad in his hand, is convalescing in FANNY's care. HE is sitting up on a chaise-longue down L, barricaded in by chairs and tables, in a lively humour and protesting vigorously. FANNY stands nearby, with an envelope in hand, waiting for the tirade to subside.)

RLS. This is worse than the boxcar. You lock me behind this grotesque stockade and throw tidbits at me as if I were an orang-utang in a menagerie.

FANNY. This is my house and what this nurse says goes. So calm down and behave. Nellie will come as usual to take dictation. But before anything else, read this!

(FANNY hands RLS the envelope, which HE scans and opens.)

RLS. It's from my father. He says he has arranged an annual allowance - *(HE looks up, eyes wide, and breathes a deep sigh of relief.)* "It might help you to support a wife and family", he says, "until the day -" It's a treaty of peace, Fanny. He writes of money, but he means forgiveness.

FANNY. He knows at last the kind of man you are.

RLS. *(Alert and eager.)* We'll go. We'll find our honeymoon shack in Silverado and then we'll go to Scotland.

FANNY. First things. first, Louis. I have to get you better. And when you are, we'll have our ceremony. I'll go see the minister. No family, no fiesta, just you and me. Now if you lie still I'll go get Nellie.

(FANNY exits through a doorway up R. RLS jumps up excitedly and breaks through the barrier of furniture. With pad and pencil in hand HE paces up and down, reciting aloud from his notes.)

RLS. "It was a bleak, uncomfortable day; but at night, by six bells, although the wind had not yet moderated, the clouds were all wrecked and blown away behind the rim of the horizon..."

(NELLIE enters R, aghast to see RLS out of his sickbed.)

NELLIE. You men! Now, Louis, get straight back to bed. Fanny will be furious.

RLS. Stop twittering! Listen, lassie, and write. "I saw Venus burning as steadily and sweetly..."

(NELLIE grabs a notebook and hurries to catch his dictation.)

RLS. " ...across the hurly-burly of the winds and waters as ever at home upon the summer woods. The engine pounded, the screw tossed out of the water with a roar, and shook the ship from end to end. The bows battled with -" ...with? *(His pacing stops abruptly.)* I need Lloyd. Where is he? I need the bosun!

(NELLIE drops everything and rushes out R to get LLOYD. In great excitement, RLS picks up the thread of his narrative.)

RLS. "The bows battled with loud reports against the billows; and as I stood in the lee-scuppers and looked up to the funnel, over my head, vomiting smoke, and the black and monstrous topsails blotted, at each lurch, a different crop of stars, it seemed as if all this trouble were a thing of small account, and -" Oh, God help me!

(HE totters, cursing, reaching for the couch, and is about to fall when LLOYD hurries in R.)

LLOYD. No, Luly! I'm coming!

(Frightened, LLOYD rushes to hold RLS and gently helps him back to his sickbed. RLS relaxes, settling back on his cushions.)

RLS. Very kind of you, laddie. You're a good chap. *(HE thrusts the notepad into LLOYD's hand.)* It was a sailing scene. I needed your suggestions.

LLOYD. *(Looking at the notepad.)* But, Luly, this isn't make-believe. This is from the "Emigrant".

RLS. Is it? You think so?

LLOYD. *(Reading.)* " ...it seemed as if all this trouble were a thing of small account, and that just above the mast reigned peace unbroken and eternal."

RLS. Yes, I remember. That is how it seemed. It was the first Sunday.

LLOYD. Oh, Luly, why are you so stubborn? All those months you wanted to live on 70 cents a day... when you'd promised to stay alive and write your best stories.

RLS. Why? Why not? No man is any use until he has dared everything. How else would I become a man? *(HE touches LLOYD's hand affectionately.)* Or either of us?

Reprise: "IF I LIVE" #24

RLS. *(Singing.)*
IF I LIVE
WE'LL SAIL OUR VESSEL TO EXOTIC LANDS,
IMAGINE CHARACTERS ON SILVER SANDS
AND LET THEM TRAP US IN THEIR SNARE;
THEN WATCH THE DRAMA OF THEIR LIVES
  UNFOLD,
WE'LL HEAR THEIR STORIES TOLD.
SO MANY FRIENDS TO SHARE
IF I LIVE.

IF I LIVE
WE'LL TAKE A FOOTPATH INTO MYSTERY,
THROUGH SILENT PASSAGES OF HISTORY
WHERE FELLOW-DREAMERS STAYED AWHILE.
WE'LL MAKE ACQUAINTANCE WITH THE
  THINGS THEY'VE DONE,
THEIR BATTLES LOST AND WON,
AND TELL THEIR TALES WITH STYLE

IF I LIVE...

(During this verse RLS and his voice have become steadily weaker. HE now appears to slip into a sleep. For a moment all is quiet. A SPOTLIGHT picks out LLOYD who watches in fear and trembling as elsewhere, from the make-believe of RLS' imagination, the stage is filled with characters from his future fiction - seafarers, highlanders, South Sea islanders, and others - and THEY take over his song.)

CHORUS.
LOOK OUT FOR CREEPING SHADOWS!
STAY STILL! WHY THE RUSH TO HIDE?

(LLOYD, restless, crouches again beside RLS' sickbed.)

CHORUS.
TAKE COURAGE FROM REALITY:

(From the chorus, a masked figure, DR. JEKYLL, steps forward.)

JEKYLL.
THERE GOES YOUR DARKER SIDE.

(On the last words the JEKYLL figure turns round, revealing - on the reverse side of the mask - the horrific face of HYDE. At the sound of skirling bagpipes, JEKYLL/HYDE vanishes. Tartan-clad figures appear, and from their midst the characters of ALAN BRECK and DAVID BALFOUR (from

"Kidnapped.")   step forward, brandishing swords and skirmishing with redcoats and other highlanders. LLOYD picks up the flageolet from beside RLS and sits at the end of the couch, breathlessly excited.)

BRECK and BALFOUR. *(Together.)*
IF I LIVE
WE'LL COMB THE HEATHER OF MY NATIVE HILLS.
WITH CUNNING WORDS AND UNEXPECTED SKILLS
WE'LL FIGHT FOR JUSTICE OR TO DIE...

(BRECK and BALFOUR, highlanders and redcoats are themselves now swept aside by an emerging band of buccaneers led, with parrot on shoulder, by LONG JOHN SILVER. The words of their old sea-song - "Fifteen men on the dead man's chest -/ Yo-ho-ho, and a bottle of rum" - are chanted in counterpoint to the final lines of the song...)

SILVER and CHORUS. *(Together.)*
AND TREASURE HUNTERS ON AN ISLAND SHORE
WILL FIND ONE STORY MORE -
THAT GOLD I HAVE TO GIVE
IF I LIVE...
IF I LIVE.

(On the last words SILVER extends a hand to LLOYD, who rises and joins the pirate band. LIGHTS dim on the fictional characters as they retreat upstage

towards the deep orange backlighting of a tropical sunset. LLOYD, silhouetted with SILVER, disappears with the pirates into the world of the author's imagination. RLS, stirring on his couch, calls out...)

RLS. Fanny!

(FANNY enters R, appearing in the SPOTLIGHT around him. SHE holds out her hand and sits with him on the couch. In the background, for fleeting moments, we can recognize two silhouetted figures - representing RLS and FANNY - standing together before a third figure, a Presbyterian Priest, apparently going through a simple marriage ceremony. The image fades, and as RLS becomes more fully awake FANNY helps him to sit up on the couch.)

RLS. I had a dream from my childhood. Please write it down. "The World is so Great and I am so Small..." In the dream I was afraid. But you know, Fanny, with you I'm very happy, and I don't feel so small.

(RLS picks up his notebook and pencil to resume writing, and we hear lingering strains of MUSIC from his song. FANNY rises quietly, smiling, and backs away to leave him in peace. RLS continues his work. HE is upright on his couch, still writing - facing R, just as he appears on the St. Gaudens medallion and the memorial plaque in St. Giles' Cathedral, Edinburgh...

...... as the final curtain falls.)

NOTES ON STAGING

The text of this Acting Edition and the associated Vocal Score incorporate revisions which followed initial productions, indoor and outdoor, under notably different staging conditions and constraints. Directions provided in the text recognize that the mechanics of staging will also necessarily vary elsewhere according to the budgets, technical facilities, and designer talents available to user companies. The directions affecting set and lighting design in particular are therefore provided as guidelines rather than as a fixed formula. The appended Furniture and Property List may also be simplified for individual productions.

Set Design. The structure and spirit of this musical call for a sustained pace in production and therefore rapid scene-changing between the multiple settings. It is assumed that in most circumstances these needs will be met by using a single, versatile main set, supplemented where necessary by furnished in-sets for specific interior scenes, drops or gauzes for certain exteriors, and ingenuity in lighting design.

Lighting Design. Directions in the text provide guidelines for lighting each scene. Where the use of spotlights is recommended for specific effects within and between scenes this is noted in the stage directions.

<u>Effects.</u>   Necessary and optional sound and visual effects are noted as such in the stage directions. Attention is drawn to the need in Act I Scene 5 for pre-recording of vocal effects by participating actors.

<u>Costume Design.</u>   Indications of principal costume requirements are given in the stage directions. Costume changes most frequently occur for chorus members in multiple roles as citizens of Edinburgh, editors/publishers, painters/models, emigrants, townsfolk of Monterey, diners and fictional characters. Among principles, a minimum of 3 costume changes each for RLS and Fanny would be necessary.

<u>Casting.</u>   Although the musical is ideally suited to performance by a large cast, it can be staged satisfactorily by a full company of 20 with doubling and/or tripling of parts and use of a smaller chorus. Doubling and tripling options include Bob/Adolfo, Wattie/Joe, Baxter/Driver, Beth/Belle/Irish Girl, Publican/Sam, 1st Constable/Wright/Simoneau, Maud/Nellie. Other permutations are possible. All extras - singing and speaking parts - can be handled by members of the chorus. Act I scene 13 can be staged without the presence of a real donkey on stage as Modestine.

CHARACTER DESCRIPTIONS

<u>NOTE:</u>   Where they occur asterisks (*) denote fictional or fictionalized characters. All others were real people whose physical and personality characteristics and relationships are well documented in the biographical literature on RLS. Where ages are given, they span the first-to-last appearances in the play.

I. PRINCIPALS

<u>Robert Louis Stevenson (RLS)</u>
Aspiring writer and "teller of tales", a reluctant law student. Only son of Thomas and Margaret, born into a famous family of engineers. Ages from 22 to 29 during the action. An Edinburgh Scot who never loses his accent and is always called "Lewis". Dark-haired, famously gaunt and tall (the "Spindleshanks" of legend), with a mellifluous baritone voice. A vivid, vital presence in company, high-spirited, eager, effervescent in conversation, with quick, nervous movements but always a certain grace. A complex, charismatic character, whose wit, charm, chivalrous manner, optimistic philosophy, sincerity and tenderness are magnetic to women and men alike. At times a romantic dreamer, at other times a serious moralist, he matures visibly during the action.

Thomas Stevenson
Father of RLS, a highly successful and respected civil engineer and pillar of Edinburgh society. Ages from 55 to 62. Scottish, with a clansman's loyalty to the Church of Scotland. Squarely and solidly built, with a strong face and mutton-chop whiskers. Stern and upright, rigid and dour, moody and melancholy, but impeccably chivalrous and with a quirky, whimsical humour. A compassionate man beneath the granite exterior.

Margaret Stevenson
Mother of RLS. Ages from 44 to 51. Scottish, from a distinguished family of clerics. Tall and slim, fair and serene. Bright, buoyant and practical, with a warm sunny disposition. Conventionally religious rather than devout, but fiercely loyal to husband Tom and indulgent towards RLS.

Bob Stevenson
Cousin of RLS, an art student and budding professional painter. Ages from 25 to 28. Scottish, Edinburgh-born. A mercurial, manic, quick-witted, and inspirational jester, with a disarming streak of vulgarity. A flamboyantly Bohemian extrovert and bon viveur, outrageously high-spirited. RLS' oldest and closest friend, and in repartee they inspire each other. A Mercutio to RLS' Romeo.

Charles Baxter
Close friend of RLS , a law student who makes good. Ages from 24 to 31. Scottish, Edinburgh-born. Big, burly, boisterous and a hard drinker, but sharp, ironic,

and with a mischievous sense of humour. Always a loyal and trusty companion to RLS, he's sufficiently canny and mature to be respected by RLS' parents. A Horatio to RLS' Hamlet.

<u>Walter ("Wattie") Simpson</u>
Friend of RLS, from a highly respected family. Ages from 29 to 32. Scottish, Edinburgh-born. Squat, stolid and amiable, with a twinkle in his eye, but slow-witted, ponderous and rather stately in his movements. Among the four student "musketeers", Sir Walter Grindlay Simpson, Bart. is usually the butt of 'others jokes.

<u>Mrs. (Frances) Sitwell</u>
A clergyman's wife, friend of Maud Babington and paramour of Sidney Colvin. Ages from 34 to 40. Of Anglo-Irish extraction, but seemingly well-bred English. Radiantly beautiful, mature, intelligent, worldly, and wise. Her joyous, gracious manner and merry laugh hide well the secrets of a troubled marriage.

<u>Sidney Colvin</u>
Professor and critic of art and literature who's done well quickly; Mrs. Sitwell's platonic younger lover who becomes RLS' editor and friend. Ages from 28 to 34. English, upper-middle class. Genial and generous-spirited, but sober, dispassionate, cautious, and correct. Instantly recognises RLS' genius and willingly becomes his patron.

<u>Fanny Vandegrift Osbourne</u>
Aspiring artist-writer, unhappy wife of Sam and mother of three. Ages from 36 to 40. American, from Indiana. Short, swarthy, and dark-complexioned, but with an original, striking beauty. A complex, frustrated woman: tough, passionate and feisty, but fun-loving and very practical. Intensely loyal to those she loves, and with no time for fools. Her eventual bond with RLS is one of shared values and interests between temperamental opposites.

<u>Sam Osbourne</u>
Fanny's husband, father of Belle and Lloyd. Ages from 40 to 44. American, from Kentucky, with a soft southern drawl. Tall, blond, and handsome, with a Van Dyke beard. Courteous and likeable, with a suave charm, but deviously selfish and an incurable womanizer.

<u>Belle Osbourne</u>
Daughter of Fanny and Sam, an art student. Ages from 17 to 21. American. Attractive, dark-complexioned and short, like her mother. A fun-loving, vivacious, adolescent, wrestling with the emotions of a teenager growing up. Idolizes her father, rows with her mother, and is amused by RLS but resents his influence.

<u>Lloyd Osbourne</u>
Son of Fanny and Sam, a schoolboy. Ages from 8 to 12. American. Fair-haired, blue-eyed and bright. Chirpy, eager, and always on the move, but slightly spoilt and vulnerable. Likes his natural father well enough but adores RLS (and in later life becomes his collaborator).

Adolfo Sanchez

A saloon-owner, engaged to Fanny's sister Nellie. Age: about 25. Spanish-American. Dark, with Latin good looks and accent. Is proud of his fruity baritone voice and plays guitar with panache. Extravagantly romantic in the macho manner. One of the most attractive, popular, and influential young men in Monterey.

Joe Strong

Aspiring portrait painter, in love with Belle. Age: about 27. American. Dark, medium build. A personable, sociable, outgoing Bohemian. A decent, well-meaning guy with a fatal flaw: he has the instability of an eventual alcoholic.

Nellie Vandegrift

Fanny's youngest sister, engaged to Adolfo. Age: early 20's (She's Belle's aunt, but her near-contemporary.) American, from Indiana. Pretty and studious, with blonde hair done in plaits. A bespectacled romantic bookworm who idolizes Fanny for her toughness and determination and RLS for his talent and charm.

II. SECONDARY CHARACTERS

First Constable (*)
A self important fellow, officious and naive.
Beth (*)
A prostitute. Young and perky, a Highland lass.

<u>Maud Babington</u>
Another cousin of RLS, a Rector's wife. Age: 28. An anglicized Scot. Sociable and hospitable, but charmingly woolly-headed.

<u>Irish Girl</u> (*)
A sweet-natured teenager from a poor home.

<u>Driver</u> (*)
A drayman. Aged: 30-50. American. Country-bred and none too bright.

<u>Jonathan Wright</u>
A bear-hunter and rough-living rancher. Age: 40's. American, from the backwoods. Bearded, well-built, with a rich bass-baritone voice. An honest, courteous, kindly man.

<u>Jules Simoneau</u>
A restaurant-owner, friend of RLS. Age: late 50's. French expatriate, not yet Americanized. A bearded, upright, benign, and worldly fellow, with a heart of gold.

<u>Modestine</u>
"A diminutive, mouse-coloured she-ass" with an awkward temperament.

III. MINOR SPEAKING/SINGING PARTS (*)

<u>Leerie</u> - A lamplighter. Middle-aged, Scottish, simple but canny.

<u>Publican</u> - Middle-aged, a Scot, bluff and jovial.

Descriptions of other extras are provided in the text where necessary.

FURNITURE AND PROPERTY LIST

ACT I, Sc. 1
On stage -
Street lamps

Off stage -
Lamp-lighters
Ladder (LEERIE)
White pamphlet (THOMAS)
Whisky bottle (BAXTER)
ACT I, Sc. 2
On stage -
Bar
  On it: 4 glasses, whisky bottle,
       small bowl
 Small table (in snug)
 Bench (in snug)

Personal: pocket-watch
(GENTLEMEN), notebook
and pencil (RLS)

Off stage -
Truncheons (CONSTABLES)
ACT I, Sc. 3
On stage -
Writing-desk
  On it: Bible (for THOMAS)
 Chair (at desk)

 Personal: white pamphlet
(THOMAS, as before)
ACT I, Sc. 4
Off stage -

Knapsack, stuffed (RLS)
ACT I, Sc. 5
On stage -
Garden seat (optional)

Off stage -
Croquet ball, 2 mallets (MAUD)
Knapsack (RLS, as before)
Croquet Mallet (MRS. SITWELL)
Stethoscope, medical bag (DOCTOR)
Couch
   On it : blanket, sheets of writing paper

Personal: notebook and pencil
(RLS, as before)
ACT I, Sc. 6
On stage -
Clubroom furniture
(optional)

Off stage -
Personal: manuscripts (RLS)
ACT I, Sc.7
On stage -
Easel
  On it: canvas painting
Small table (by easel)
  On it: painting materials,
       wine bottle, 2 glasses
Stool or chair (MODEL)

Personal: artist's palette,
       paintbrush (BOB)

Off stage-
Knapsack, bottle of champagne (RLS)
Camping gear, including tent,
sleeping bags, pans, etc. (WATTIE)

3 suitcases (SAM, MAID)
2 hats (BELLE, LLOYD)
Fishing-rod (LLOYD)
Painting materials, including
sketchpad, brush/crayons (FANNY)
Easels, canvases (PAINTERS, optional)
Dining-table
9 chairs
Wine-bottle (BOB)
Steaming bowl (MAID)
Food & wine as required
ACT I, Sc. 8
On stage -
2 canoes
  In them: 2 paddles

Off stage -
Knapsack (RLS, as before)
ACT I, Sc. 9
On stage -
White umbrellas
Easels
  On them: canvases
Stools or chairs
Easel & stool (for FANNY)
Small Table
  On it: sketching material
  (for FANNY, BELLE)
Sketchpad & crayons (FANNY)

Off stage -
Fishing-rod (LLOYD, as before)
Large fish (WATTIE)

Personal: notebook and pencils
(RLS, as before)
ACT I, Sc.10
On stage -

(Set as for Scene 3)
ACT I, Sc.11
On stage -
(Set as for Scene 6)
ACT I, Sc. 12
Off stage -
3 suitcases (FANNY, BELLE, LLOYD,
as before in Scene 7)
2 small gift packages (RLS)
ACT I, Sc.13
Off stage -
Knapsack (RLS, as before)
Camping gear and/or packsaddle
with stuffed paniers
ACT I, Sc.14
On stage -
Small desk
  On it: book (for LLOYD), writing
  paper, envelope, pen (for FANNY)
Easel (for BELLE)
  On it: sketchpad and pencil
  (for BELLE)

Off stage-
Letter (RLS)
2 sealed envelopes (RLS)
Letter (THOMAS)
Letter (THOMAS)
Knapsack (RLS, as before)
Portmanteau (RLS)
Books (RLS)
ACT I, Sc. 15
On stage -
Bunks and/or mattresses
(for PASSENGERS)
  On them: blankets, belongings
Small table (for RLS aboard ship)
Chair (beside table)

Off stage -
Knapsack and portmanteau
(RLS, as before)
Fiddle (FIDDLER)
Chessboard (MALE PASSENGER,
optional)
Crutch (ONE-LEGGED PASSENGER)
6 volumes, strap bound (RLS)

Personal: notebook and pencil
(RLS, as before)
ACT II, Sc. 1
On stage -
End of railcar, with steps visible
Scrubby bush
2-wheeled cart, with harness &
reins visible

Off stage -
Knapsack and portmanteau
(RLS, as before)
6 volumes (RLS as before)
Guitar (ADOLFO)
Filled whisky tumbler (JOE)
2 filled brandy glasses

Personal: purse, coins (RLS),
holster, pistol (ADOLFO)
ACT II, Sc. 2
On stage - Dresser
  On it: Kitchen utensils, pots and
  pans, tray with cups and plate of
  cookies
Small tables
Chairs
Sofa
  On it: cushions
Sketchpad and pencil (BELLE)